DOLLYGAL PEACOCK AND THE SERPENT

Conquering Ego... The return to the Extraordinary

by

Darlene Cannon

Dollygal Peacock and the Serpent
Conquering Ego... The return to the Extraordinary

Copyright © 2023 by Darlene Cannon

My name is Darlene cannon. I am a visionary on a mission.

I give all credit to God for all of the beautiful, mundane, and mystical thoughts that flow through my mind daily.

These thoughts form into a story. The stories are written down.

Then the helping hands come together,(publishers,designers,editors etc.) and bring the vision into physical form.

Thank you, to all of the talented,unique and humble helping hands in the world...

Be the peace...Be the Love...Bepeacelove...!

About the book

"MANTRA"

This story is about Love, hope and charity...

Growing up and excepting ourselves exactly as we are...

Knowing that anything is possible, and nothing is impossible...

Knowing that hope can heal the world...

Knowing that everyone has his own unique
way of creating peace on earth...

Believing in oneself is possible...

Having faith in what we believe ourselves to be is not impossible!

Trusting ourselves and knowing that we can acually be
something far greater than we ever imagined is fathomable...

Finding out who we are and discovering our true purpose in life,

can take us on a fascinating and mystical journey
into the world of enlightenment...

Get prepared to follow Dollygal, Peacock, and the Serpent on
their fascinating journey into the world of enlightenment!

Be the peace...Be the love...Bepeacelove!

ACKNOWLEDGMENTS

We extend our heartfelt appreciation to everyone
who contributed to the making of this book.

Written by Darlene Cannon

Illustrated by Sonny Nicholas

Edited By: Goldman Agency

CONTENTS

Chapter I

VICTORY IN THE GARDEN

*D*ollygal slowly wakes up to the chatter of people talking outside the window besides her bed. Below professor Boo and Mr. Protege are explaining why the "Victory Garden" is bursting into the light!*

"If it seems as though, the garden is now bursting into magnificent light; that is because you are now accepting yourself as an extraordinary person. When this phenomenon occurs within you, this means that the hero within you has now risen. Therefore, fear no longer resides within you. The key to living extraordinarily, as you are in this moment, is to always remember who you are and who you are not!"

Professor Boo, points his finger at everyone as he speaks. Then Mr. Protege continues the teaching.

"You are not fearful because it has been proven that fear cannot back up its claim to have the power to hurt, confuse or destroy you. Fear can convince the ordinary person that it's in control, and you must become subservient to its presence. We have seen this acted by Laszlo, and we have also seen him destroyed by a greater power than himself. Dollygal demonstrated the extraordinary by knowing that she was divinely connected to greater power than Laszlo."

"I could not have explained that any better my friend." Professor Boo joyfully says.

"Finally, I'm free to be extraordinarily me. Romain shouted while wiggling her layers of green leaves."

"I can't wait for that handsome Mr. Godfrey to see me shimmering, and sparkling like golden dust; fresh from the universe." Miss Lottie cheerfully says.

"I can't believe that last month he's finally gone. It feels like shackles have been released from my mind." Aphrodite stretches out her leaves and gives a sigh of relief.

"I think he was misunderstood and wounded." says Anatolia.

"Dear sister of mine, I do not think you recovered from the blackout moment you suffered." Romain says.

"In other words, darling, you are still in the dark." Miss Lottie replied.

Professor Boo brushes his hands across Anatolia's big bushy leaves and replies,

"Perhaps, it is yourself who feels misunderstood and wounded!"

Meanwhile upstairs, Dollygal prepares for the day, as her reflection in the mirror, reveals her in a new way!

Now, Dollygal opens the closets doors to look at all the colorful dresses. While deciding which one to wear, an orange dress suddenly falls onto the ground. Dollygal picks it up and twirls around in front of a large oval-shaped mirror.

"Oh! Mystical! Mystical me! You're the perfect dress for me to wear today."

"Perfect for you Dollygal, but not for me. The voice from the mirror echoed.

"Who said that?! Is anyone else in my room?!" Dollygal looks around her room.

"Oh! What a perfect Princess you will become. Pardon me, I mean Queen. You fight for the greater good by destroying my people." The voice spoke sarcastically.

Dollygal looks directly into the mirror.

"Why don't you show yourself? Let me see who you really are."

"Ha... huh..., I forgot how naive you can be. Silly girl, you're looking at who I really am. I... AM... YOU!"

"No, you are not." Dollygal said sternly.

"How can you say that? I look like you, I sound like you, and even carries the burden of your namesake, eve!"

"The reflection I see in this mirror may look like me, but the spirit is surely of another. You will never be me." Dollygal's eyes flicker with light as she speaks.

"What a clever girl you are. So clever you must know that I am taking over now just like in the precious "Great Garden" of yours. I am Lily, your dark side and I have my own agenda. Ha... Ha... Ha...!"

"I know that Laszlo is defeated and therefore, so are you. The minds of the people in Lovely Ville are now liberated. But we are also aware that the defeated ones, such as you, cannot accept the final act that has taken place; but you will very soon."

"You could never overpower me because there is no more division. The illusion of separation is defeated with Laszlo—the knowing and the knowledge of the one great power within us all, has been revealed. Laszlo is now defeated by this great power." Dollygal replied.

"I would say that you are smarter than you look. You are correct, I do not accept the final act that has taken place. I have exactly three days to change your mind from believing that you are connected to the great creator. All I must do is make you doubt yourself once, then I will emerge stronger than ever!" says Lily.

Now Dollygal's hands begin to rise, then her eyes begin to sparkle with light. The mirror begins to shake, and with a belly full of laughter her mouth opens wide and the voice cries out—God God God !!!

The mirror shook rapidly as the colorful winds from the North, South, East, and West—wraps Lily up. They gently carry her away within the mirror.

Then the voice whispers in Dollygal's ear,

"When the hero rises; Fear will no longer reside.

"You have returned to the Extraordinary."

Chapter II

THE AWAKENING OF
THE SERPENT

Serpent frantically rises from his bed frightened and confused by a dream. He takes a clear glass from the table next to the bed and splashes himself in the face with water.

"Oh, what a nightmare! No it was not. I am remembering that tragic night with Mother and Father."

"Sitting up on the side of his bed, he covers his face with his hands..."

"Serpent are you OK?" Godfrey and I are waiting for you downstairs. We have lots of things to discuss about the opening of "The School of Intention".

"I'm having nightmares about Mother and Father." says Serpent.

"Get dressed and come downstairs Serpent. We can talk about this over breakfast with Godfrey." Says Peacock

"Indeed, I do smell the most magnificent aroma of fresh ginger tea with freshly baked bread, and lightly glazed Shank ham with olives, parsley, and a hint of Rosemary."

"Wait a minute! Fresh apples from the "Great Garden" are in the baked bread?! Oh, how the heavenly aroma permeates the entire house." Serpent says with his hands clenched together.

Peacock glares at the Sssssserpent and says:

"Snap out of it, sssssserpent! Ha... Ha... Ha...

Let's go eat some of this food with this heavenly aroma... Ha... Ha... Ha..."

Serpent shrugs his shoulders and folds his arms together.

"I am not amused by your misguided sense of charm, brother of mine. Why do you need to constantly say my name like that?"

"I have always said your name like that whenever you bother me in some way. Now you're all sensitive about it?!" says Peacock.

"Oh no! On the contrary, I am not sensitive at all! I can only imagine how you feel when I talk about your bird droppings around the house now and then."

"It must strike a nerve with you, eventually making you feel uncomfortable in your own skin." says Serpent.

"OK Serpent, I get the message loud and clear. You are right my brother; we are not the same as we were before. Now we are embracing our likeness, and we have more in common than I ever realized." says Peacock.

"Brother of mine, do you know what this moment is about?"

"This is a universal teaching moment; and we must use it for the opening night at the "School of Intention". The awareness of our own self, at the moment it is occurring." says Serpent.

"Let us share this enlightening moment with Godfrey. I'm sure he will enjoy this as much as we are." says Peacock.

Peacock and Serpent begin walking excitedly down the hallway, passing by the photos of their Mother and Father on the wall. As they walked down the spiral gold staircase, a strong breeze began to blow and then lifted them off the ground. Peacock and Serpent began holding onto the staircase as their bodies dangle in the wind. Suddenly a deep voice emerges from the wind saying... IT IS DONE!!!

Godfrey hurries to meet Peacock and Serpent at the staircase from the room downstairs.

"Are you both OK?" says Godfrey.

"Yes, I'm OK. Serpent, are you OK?" asks Peacock.

"Yes, I'm OK." Replies Serpent.

"Let's check on Dollygal." says Serpent.

They hurry upstairs running down the long hallway, finally ending at Dollygal's room. Bursting through the white double door; stumbling over one another, they frantically searched the room for Dollygal.

"Dollygal, where are you?" "Where are you?" Peacock yelled out loudly.

"I'm here behind the closet door, brother Peacock." The voice of the garden delivered another message. I mean the voice. I mean the breath... the source... it is done!

"Yes. We heard it." says Peacock.

"No, we heard—It is Done," Dollygal heard something else, says Godfrey.

"What did you say a moment ago, dear child?" says the Serpent.

"I don't remember what I said a moment ago, brother Serpent."

"That's OK, Dollygal. Let's go downstairs, and have a bit of breakfast and check on Professor Boo and Mr. Protégé.

When the time is right, then we will all know what you have spoken." says Godfrey.

"The message from the Garden is noticeably clear. It has been a Victory in the Garden and for us all. Let nothing else convince us of anything other than this truth, that we now believe."

"Let us retreat to the study room and share ideas for the "School of Intention" says Godfrey.

"Oh, I hope our tea and delightful breakfast has not been blown away! I was so... so looking forward to eating." says the Serpent.

Peacock picks up Dollygal and carries her downstairs with Godfrey and Serpent. As they get downstairs, a moaning sound is heard from the outside patio leading to the "Great Garden".

"Help!"

"Wait... wait... I hear something..." says Godfrey.

"I hear it too... I think it's coming from outside the door." says Serpent.

"Helllp !!!... We are buried out here on the patio. Please help us." Professor Boo cries out.

"I will take Dollygal into the study room and gather breakfast, while you and Godfrey rescue Professor Boo and Mr. Protégé." Peacock says to Serpent.

Out on the patio, Professor Boo and Mr. Protege are covered in tree debris that had fallen from the great winds.

"Ooooh...! Please, will someone help us? We are under here..."

"I see you Professor Boo, grab my hand and I'll pull you out. Are you OK?" asks Godfrey.

"Yes, I seem to be OK! No broken bones or bruises. I could use a strong cup of ginger tea." replies Professor Boo.

"Quickly Godfrey, help me remove those tree branches. I think Mr. Protege is unconscious." says Serpent

"Pull him out and lay him down on the patio table." says Godfrey

"Oh no... not my best friend in the world! Please help him, you've got to help him." says Professor Boo.

"Will you please calm down, he's awakening slowly." says Serpent.

"Mr. Protege can you hear me? Can you see Godfrey?"

"What about Professor Boo, can you see him?" says Serpent.

Looking around in a dizzy daisy haze Mr. Protege sees his best friend.

"Professor Boo... is that you?" says Mr. Protégé.

"Yes... yes, it is I. Are you OK my friend?"

"I feel great and full of gratitude to all of you for feeling such love for me, even you Serpent." says Mr. Protégé

"Why? Of course, we all love you Mr. protégé. We're family now." says Godfrey.

"Thank you, Sir. Now, I know it because I felt it from each of you while laying down on the table, and it woke me up."

"What woke you up?" says Serpent.

"I think Mr. Protege is telling us that "Love" woke him up. The one living presence that connects us all." says Godfrey.

"The great breath of life... that is what blew through this house and live in the Garden." says Professor Boo

"That is what communicates with our dear little sister." says Serpent. (As he lowers his head, then covers his eyes with his hands.)

"Serpent... are you OK?"

"No, I'm not Godfrey. I feel very dizzy perhaps a glass of water will help." (Serpent then falls forward onto the ground.)

"Oh no... Mr. Serpent, please wake up. Perhaps all of this is just too much for him." says Mr. Protege

"I think he will be OK. Let's carry him into the study room and join Peacock and Dollygal." says Godfrey

They carry Serpent from the patio, through the dining area, slightly down the hallway, and into the study room where they lay his body on the sofa.

"What happened to Serpent?" asks Peacock.

"He just fainted in front of us a minute ago." says Godfrey.

Dollygal leans close to Serpent and speaks into his ear. Peacock, Godfrey, Professor Boo, and Mr. Protege all gather around Serpent.

"Brother Serpent, wake up! It's OK to remember what happened. You are forgiven brother Serpent... wake up!"

"Oh my... where am I? What happened?"

"You fainted and now you are in Father's study room. We're all here with you, my brother." says Peacock

Serpent looks at each of his family and friends. My brother, Professor Boo, Mr. Protégé, and Dollygal. Dear sister of mine, "Oh my... how you look like our Mother!"

"Did you hear me, Brother Serpent?" Dollygal says.

"What are you talking about, dear sister?"

"You are forgiven."

"What am I forgiven for?"

"You are forgiven for whatever it is that you don't want to remember." says Dollygal

"How do you know this?"

"The voice in the "Great Garden," brother Serpent."

"I think Serpent has had quite an experience so far today and probably needs to eat. Let's talk about this later Dollygal." says Godfrey

"Yes indeed. Mr. Protege and I took the initiative and brought in the food from the parlor—the perfectly cooked Shank ham glistens with honey and herbs, olives, parsley and a hint of Rosemary freshly picked from the Garden. Homemade butter biscuits, cinnamon apple muffins, (apples picked from the Garden) with Peach and strawberry sorbet.

Freshly scrambled eggs and chives, fresh mixed fruit with homemade cream, and ginger tea. Everything was all still in its original place and wasn't touched at all by that enormous gust of wind that blew through the house." says Professor Boo.

"That is how the voice speaks Professor Boo." says Dollygal.

"I stand corrected by the child. It is not just a gust of wind; but it is how the voice speaks and that is very powerful." says Professor Boo.

"Let's eat. Then we will process our meeting about the School of Intention." says Peacock.

Chapter III

"THE BEGINNING OF ALL GREAT POSSIBILITIES"

Four Angels are looking out for doubt...

In all four directions...an Angel watches out for doubt within, "The Great Garden."

Angel of the north sees the doubt...

Angel of the south expose the doubt...

Angel of the east corrects doubt...

Angel of the west transforms doubt...

Angel of the **North** sees the doubt...Then corrects all misunderstandings...

Angel of the south expose the doubt...by questioning all negative thought...

Angel of the east corrects doubt...By showing positive affects in good or bad...

Angel of the west transforms doubt...by reveiling the Truth and Love in all things...

Voice of "The Great Garden"

———————⚬✕⚬———————

"Meeting will now take place and all ideas are welcome. I'd like to initiate Dollygal into our group. I think she will be able to give much insight into what we are going to achieve in the School of Intention."

"Everyone is in agreement, Peacock?" says Godfrey.

"Dollygal, we all welcome you into the committee. Do you have anything to say to the group?"

"This feels like the beginning of all great possibilities, and the chance to be yourself..." Dollygal speaks with a big smile.

"That is a very mature statement for a child." says professor Boo.

"I love it! Especially the "be yourself-part." says Mr. protege.

"Indeed, I see we will be learning a lot from our dear little sister. Wouldn't you say Peacock?"

Peacock stands with arms folded in front of him and clears his throat before speaking:

"Absolutely! In fact, I think you just gave me a subject to talk about in my opening speech—The beginning of all great possibilities."

That is exactly what we are doing. I will take notes of our ideas, then we can put a curriculum together. So far, we have "the beginning of all great possibilities" and "be yourself," says Godfrey.

"Oh Peacock, do add the moment of Divine Truth you and I shared in my room. We shared a moment of realizing the awareness of ourselves at the moment it was occurring. Then we embraced the good, which is more difficult to do."

"Now you're onto something Mr. Serpent. May I ask, how did that make you feel when you embrace the good?" says Professor Boo.

"As if I was weakening myself, yet I felt stronger than I had ever felt before. I felt this happen when Dollygal and I faced Laszlo. I've been feeling it ever since. I am remembering the love Mother had for us, Peacock. I was always jealous of you, because I thought she loved you more than me! But now, I know differently, my brother. She loves me just as much. Mother had a way of understanding us as we were. With an abundance of unconditional love for us both. Not to mention the undying love she had for Father a great philosopher and scientist.

Taught me – about music and great philosophers; and taught you to be a loyal military protector. I am aware that Love is the greatest power that there ever was – that there is – and will ever be."

"My brother, the Serpent – you remember that phrase from Mother when she would come into our room when we were afraid and cast out the monsters that we thought were lurking around. I remember the softest and warm feeling the room would have after those words were spoken."

"Are you aware that you called me the Serpent, differently this time brother of mine?" Serpent says with a grin.

"I spoke from the heart this time Serpent. A place of love for my brother. I am also having an overwhelming feeling that you, my brother, need to teach at the School of Intention."

"I never thought of anything that could be beneficial coming from you Mr. Serpent, but I do now." says Professor Boo.

"I concur. I agree. Because Mr. Serpent represented everything that was the opposite of good; or you were just always negative and creepy about stuff." says Mr. Protégé.

The Serpent clears his throat and raises his left eyebrow higher than the other.

"Ha... Ha... Haaa!!! What do you think Dollygal?" Godfrey says as he picks her up off the ground.

"Oh Mystical! Mystical me! I am so happy to see my brothers together like this and embracing in a big hug." says Dollygal.

"I knew when she started with the mystical, mystical me... something highly unlikely was coming next," Serpent speaks sarcastically.

"I'm willing to do it... if you are Serpent." says Peacock.

"I could be wrong, but I'm feeling an embrace of some sort about to happen any moment. I do not want to overthink this moment, truly I do not." Serpent speaks nervously and sarcastically.

"Serpent, I'm going to hug you. We have not embraced since we were small children. But, if you are not up to this happening, then I will understand. I do not want to overthink this moment, truly I don't... ha... ha... ha..."

The powerful embracing hug between Peacock and the Serpent created a circular light that swirled around them, up and out the window, down through the blades of green grass in the Garden, passing through the pink, yellow, white, and red roses, swirling above the clearwater in the lake, rising upwards into the air tickling the tree leaves along the way and finally dispersing itself into specks of light into the middle of the unending and forever expanding "Great Garden".

The inhabitants of the Garden—"The tree people" share the land with many others. The "frolly lollies" have made their home within the forever flowing waterfalls, that seemingly fall from the sky and are heard throughout the town.

The four angelic friends are protectors from the North, South, East, and West. They look out for any thoughts of doubt that may arise in the "Great Garden". Doubt causes the Garden to disappear.

The living waters lake teaches people how to be themselves, by revealing a reflection of their true selves. This is a part of themselves, that they've yet to know.

The vegetable patch has expanded into a wide variety of green leafy nourishing healthy food. Beans, squash, asparagus, cabbage, lettuce, kale, zucchini, fresh fruit strawberries, peaches, apricots, lemons, oranges, olives, and every other food that anyone could think of.

The grandest tree of all time, stands in the very center of the "Great Garden". The apples are of all colors and like all the fruits and vegetables in the "Great Garden". Everything grows all year round and is always ripe and ready for picking. The "Great Garden" is a living Garden.

The valley of the tree people has expanded into a large crystal White City. Their original king of the village handed over full power to Megan-spirit bear and Morgan-truth bear. He now resides quietly, alone, and as a humble servant around the city. Different groups of people in the village are united and are growing stronger as they embrace the differences in one another. The vibration of energy is elevated in the village. Their physical appearance now emanates multiple colors surrounding them.

Music and dance are part of the old original language of the village – once ignored and discarded, but now carried forward by the elders. They now embrace, honor and accept these sacred practices along with the young generational music and dance that has emerged within the village. The fusion of the two has created a vibrational sound that has never been heard before!

Lavender and white lilies permeate the air. While Art and Poetry are on the minds and tongues of every villager. Creativity is the new normal.

The Great Divine Mother Earth and Great Divine Father are acknowledged within the village as the power source of all lives. The tree people believe their humble beginnings began with this life source—the great power that ever was – that there is – and will ever be.

This power source dwells within everyone in the village, and because of it, they are growing and learning, how to be themselves.

The United Kingdom's – Megan-spirit bear and Morgan-truth bear lead the ceremony and announces something new to the village...

"Today in our village, we are living the prophecy handed down from our ancestors. We are all doing our part in this Universal Divine Plan." says Morgan-truth bear.

"We thank our family and friends, Dollygal, Peacock and the Serpent, Godfrey, Professor Boo and Mr. Protégé, and many others in the Garden.

Because of the efforts on their part, we're experiencing another addition to the "Great Garden", of which our Tree Village is now a part of." says Megan-spirit bear.

"I asked all of you to stay aware of the "Awakening of the Gift" that we have received. So, please carry on with your daily activities. We have freshly cut lumber, tools, art supplies, fresh vegetables from the Garden, and newly carved instruments for our musicians. And for our dancers, you will find new material bought over from the townspeople boutique store." says Morgan-truth bear.

"Morgan-truth bear, I am so pleased with our people using their Gifts. Our village is beautiful, our people are in unity." says Megan-spirit bear, as she hugs her brother tightly.

"Megan-spirit bear, we still have a challenge to deal with and it is coming our way very soon." says Morgan-truth bear.

Morgan-truth bear takes out a folded piece of paper from his pants pocket.

"The king gave me this paper. He's had it since the beginning of the village. It was handed down to him from his ancestors. He thinks it's time we put it to use."

The prophecy reads: The Shadow Ones controlled the lower mundane world. In order to protect their power and position, a curse was put into place, in case, they were ever to be destroyed. According to our ancestors, the people hold the key to the final victory or destruction. The people were hated by the Shadow Ones, because people were given authority by the Great Divine Mother and Divine Father.

The people were tricked by the Shadow Ones, and lost connection with the divine source. Little by little the Shadow Ones manipulated the thoughts and soon created a world that would follow their direction.

The belief of the people empowered the Shadow Ones. The people were presented with new ideas and new ways to view themselves and one another. Soon these ways became the way of life, and they never knew anything other.

The Shadow Ones blended and became a big part of the people and their society, which they are now known as EGO. The curse is a belief (held by the EGO) that the people would never be able to accept or remember their power of Authority. A three-day time limit will be put on the people to believe or not believe in themselves.

Megan-spirit bear takes the paper from Morgan-truth bear...

"So, Liaison and Laszlo were created by the Ego, and destroyed by love."

"Exactly. So what we believe about ourselves is very important, and what we don't believe about ourselves is very important." says Morgan-truth bear.

"So even though our village and people are doing well, we could be doing even better?!" says Megan-spirit bear.

"According to the prophecy, that would be part of the final new addition coming into the "Great Garden" says Morgan-truth bear.

As Morgan-truth bear speaks, something in the sky catches Megan-spirit bear's attention.

"Morgan-truth bear, did you see a shadow move across the sky?"

"No. But did you feel the ground shake?"

Slowly the ground began to shake. Rumbling sounds move through the village quickly and are dispersed throughout the grounds of the entire Garden. Rumbling and rolling under the Earth; lifting every plant, tree, and blade of grass.

Forcing its way through the "Great Garden" then bursting through the back door of the castle house, rolling and rumbling into the study room knocking Dollygal out of the chair and onto the floor.

"Dollygal, are you all right?" says Godfrey.

"Yes, I'm OK. Did you hear that?" she says as she wipes off her dress.

"Who could miss all of that rumbling and rolling." says Serpent.

"We would all like to know what it was, and where it came from." says Peacock.

"I think I have an explanation for what we all just experienced. It is the beginning of something new or more. It's a part of what we encountered earlier, but more in physical form." says Professor Boo.

"Well, thank you for the insightful thought. We would have never ever figured that out!" Serpent says sarcastically.

"Serpent, let's work together please." says Peacock.

Dollygal joyfully twirls around saying, "The Return to the Extraordinary." That is what I heard when the rumbling rolled into the study room with us."

"I guess we'll have to wait and see what that means. In the meantime, we have great ideas for the opening of the School of Intention. The remodeling, painting, and new fixtures are all completed in our new building. So, it's all ready for tomorrow's opening ceremony." says Godfrey.

"Great! I made up a list of assignments for each of us to do. Serpent, one of your assignments needs attending to, right now. The school sign is the last to be delivered today. Get there and show them where to put it." says Peacock.

"I am on my way, as soon as I grab my top hat and maybe my new overcoat, and a fresh cigar."

Mr. Protege interrupts. May I end the meeting?"

I always wanted to do that. It would make me so happy if I could, please... please... Can I, huh?"

"Please do my friend. You are very welcome to do so." says Professor Boo.

"I now declare this meeting adjourned!!!"

Chapter IV

COME AS YOU ARE

The Serpent arrives in the nearby town. People greeted him warmly, as he exits the carriage in front of the "School of Intention."

"Good day, Mr. and Mrs. Cleary. I see you both are up and about early this morning." Serpent says while taking off his top hat.

"Yes, indeed it is. I'm expecting the sign to be delivered anytime now."

"Indeed, we're all working together here in town to make sure everything is just perfect, Sir. My wife and I have been instructed by your brother Mr. Peacock, to organize and distribute different tasks for the people here in town. I'll let my wife explain the wonderful ideas the women have been working on."

"Oh! We have been working with the seamstress shop and have created new uniforms for the children. The tree people have made a new blackboard for Mrs. Engirdle and today they're bringing fresh apples from the garden for the celebrations."

"All of that sounds simply marvelous, Mrs. Cleary. But I do believe I'm getting just a faint aroma of apples and freshly baked bread." says Serpent.

"Oh... Oh... Mr. Serpent (she giggles), yes, that is the baker getting started with fresh bread and freshly churned butter for the midday brunch. Thanks to the tree people bringing fresh apples from the garden, we will be making apple pies for the school opening tomorrow."

"As you can see Sir, everything is in order. Oh, Miss Engirdle will be here shortly to discuss her classroom curriculum. Good day, Sir." says Mr. Cleary as he tips his hat to the Serpent.

Serpent continues his short walk down the gravel street leading to the school. Next to the door, an unknown tree makes himself known—

"Long time no see... my friend." says the tree.

The Serpent looks to his left and then his right.

"Who said that? Where are you?"

"I am here Serpent, and I am your friend from long ago. My name is Sycamore!"

"It's a talking tree named Sycamore. I must be hearing things! No, no... let me correct myself. We are now elevated in a higher vibration. This moment would be totally normal to my little sister." The Serpent rubs his forehead.

"You're right about that Serpent. She was born knowing the Truth, remember?

You was there with your mother under the Sycamore tree—that would be me."

The Serpent lowers his head and looks down.

"I do remember the old Sycamore tree, I used to play under every day. I also remember my mother giving birth to my little sister under the Sycamore tree in the pouring rain."

"No time to hang your head low Serpent. The Shadow Ones are here to prevent the elevated vibration that the garden and all of you have attained." said Sycamore.

"But my little sister defeated Liaison and Laszlo. How could the Shadow Ones prevent our elevation?"

"They rely on all of you to doubt your own power in your own victory of being elevated out of an Ego perspective." says Sycamore.

The Serpent hangs his head down and covers his face.

"So now what happens Sycamore?"

"You either believe in yourselves or you believe what the Shadow Ones believe you to be. It's up to all of you." says Sycamore.

"Oh dear, here comes the schoolteacher Miss Engirdle. The poor woman has been a wreck since losing her son. I think it's best if you kept quiet Sycamore, as she approaches. I hope you are not offended?" says the Serpent.

"Ah, good day Mrs. Engirdle, let's go inside and have a look at your curriculum for the children." says Serpent.

"Oh, but of course Mr. Serpent, but first I must say hello to my old friend Sycamore."

"How lovely you look today Miss Engirdle. That yellow dress and hat blend beautifully with your red hair." says Sycamore.

"Oh my! Thank you, Sycamore. You always know exactly what to say." she giggles.

"Sorry to break up the chitter chatter, but Mrs. Engirdle has business to attend to." says the Serpent as he guides her into the school.

"Oh, my goodness everything looks wonderful Mr. Serpent. It was such a great idea to combine my classroom into this building—The School of Intention." says Miss Engirdle

"Yes, well our intention is to blend all teachings together. So, the curriculum for the children is very important." says Serpent.

"Well, my ideas were inspired by Dollygal. It's about being yourself. I do believe this will fit in perfectly with the teachings Mr. Peacock is sharing." says Mrs. Engirdle.

"I agree, it sounds like... a great fit into the school's agenda. Please tell me about your ideas." says Serpent.

"Dollygal's life has been about self-awareness of her own abilities and inabilities; wouldn't you say, Sir?"

"Yes, indeed I would say so."

"Well, being yourself seems to be the key to living in the vibration we are currently experiencing. So, this year's curriculum will focus on being yourself."

"Absolutely marvelous Miss Engirdle! Continue working at what you have started, and we will see you tomorrow for the opening. I am quite sure my dear brother will love your ideas for the school, this year."

"I will be here promptly Sir. Oh, it looks like the delivery man is here Mr. Serpent." "I'll let them in on my way out."

"Hello, we're here to install your sign Sir. Would you like it on the front door or on top of the building?" "The Sycamore tree, likes it on top of the entrance door."

"Listen to my instructions, not the Sycamore tree's." The Serpent says as he steps outside the door.

"Hmmmm, directly over the door please, and leave your bill in the mailbox when you're done. We will pay you promptly."

"Thank you, Mr. Serpent."

"Good day sir," says the Sycamore tree.

"Good day Sycamore!" says the Serpent.

Meanwhile back at home, Dollygal is greeted with a surprise in her room!

"Hey, the surprise gift was just delivered for you Dollygal, I kept it on your bed." says Peacock.

"You were in my room, brother Peacock? Did you see anything?"

"Nothing but your regular room. Bed and closet and window and stuff like that. Is there a problem?" He says with a concerned look on his face.

"Oh, no brother Peacock, I just didn't want you to see anything that's not supposed to be there." Dollygal twitters her fingers behind her back.

"Oh, I see. Your room was clean, and you think I didn't notice. Good job Dollygal."

"Thanks for noticing, brother Peacock."

"All the reason for you to have the gift that is waiting for you. Run along upstairs."

"I can't wait to see what it is." says Dollygal.

Chapter V

CONQUERING EGO

*D*ollygal *runs up the spiral staircase, down the hallway, and bursts through the double white doors, leading into her bedroom. She jumps on the bed where the package is wrapped in the beautiful white box with red, yellow, green, orange, blue and purple bowls. She opens it quickly.*

"Wow! Oh mystical! !Mystical me! A Red dress – as red as the apples on the trees and sparkles like stars in the sky." she says while trilling around.

"Oh, what a pretty Red dress. Could I wear it sometimes?" "Haha, that is a joke of course. That is so not my style." says Lily as she emerges from the mirror and onto Dollygal room.

"What are you doing here? How are you able to come into my room? Why don't you like this Red dress?"

"No, I don't care if you don't like my Red dress." says Dollygal as she wipes her forehead.

"I almost made you doubt didn't I Princess?" Lily stands with both hands-on her hips.

"Your angelic friends cannot keep me away, as long as I am with the Shadow Ones." Says Lily. "Who are the Shadow Ones?" says Dollygal

"Of course, you would not know who dislikes you the most ha... ha... ha..." Lily circles around Dollygal as she speaks.

"The Shadow Ones have been empowering people in village for an awfully empowering our people for an awfully long time. Now they are being destroyed because of you. Our way of life is diminishing, because of your love, hope, and charity universal heart. Thoughts like yours do not belong in our world."

"Why hasn't anyone seen them before?" says Dollygal.

"They have been behind the clouds and witnessed your birth. They intermingle with people's thoughts and help them to understand the differences between themselves. Your mother and father knew them quite well. Oh, but of course, you would not know anything about that. But I do says Lily.

"What do you know about my birth?" says Dollygal.

"Your birth was a mistake, and you are the one responsible for your mother and father's death. Yes, it is true Dollygal. You are not a savior you are a curse." says Lily.

Dollygal stands up to Lily—

"Stop Lily, you speak the opposite of the truth, just like Liaison and Laszlo. My brother Serpent used to speak the same, but now, he does not anymore."

"My birth was not a mistake; I am meant to be here." says Dollygal as she moves closer to Lily.

"I am meant to be here too. I was born into the family of the Shadow Ones, and I am the opposite of you. So, when you start to doubt and your people start to doubt their own power; then I will complete my mission for my people." says Lily.

"Lovelyville will not doubt their power this time Lily. They have already accomplished unity." says Dollygal.

Lily and Dollygal disagree.

"They have not accomplished unity." Says Lily

"They have accomplished unity." says Dollygal.

"They have not...

"They have too...

a knock at the bedroom door startled Dollygal and Lily.

Peacock makes his presence known as he opens the door.

"Dollygal, did you like your gift?

"I love my new Red dress brother Peacock, thank you." Dollygal stands by her bed.

"I'm glad you like it. You can wear it to the school opening tomorrow. Serpent and I will match our attire to your Red dress. This was his idea of course. You know how he loves to dress up."

"By the way. Were you speaking to someone before I came in?" asks Peacock.

"What do you mean? There is no one here but me, Myself and I... ha... ha... ha... ha..."

"Well, I know how you have special friends that visit you sometimes. Serpent and I completely support you exactly as you are Dollygal. There's nothing that we will not understand and nothing we will not believe. We were wrong to try to change you before. We are all uniquely special, and you have helped us all to see that." Peacock picks up Dollygal in his arms as he speaks.

"I have something to tell you, brother Peacock. I was speaking to someone before you came into my room."

"Who are you speaking to Dollygal?" says Peacock, as he puts her down.

"Lily is her name. She came out of the mirror and now she and the shadow people are trying to stop us and the people of Lovely Ville and the "Great Garden".

Peacock sits on the end of the bed -

"Wait, wait a minute. Dollygal, I'm trying to keep up with your stories."

"I have got to speak the truth and I cannot doubt anything brother Peacock, neither can you or brother Serpent or any of our friends. We have got to continue to believe what we have already experienced." Dollygal speaks with tears in her eyes

"We are believing now Dollygal. They are changing and the School of Intention is opening with new classes. So, what more can we do?" says brother Peacock.

"But Lily says the shadow people do not believe people could ever really accept their true power. And because of that, they will lose it." says Dollygal.

"Dollygal, perhaps you had a very vivid dream." says Peacock.

Remember what you said brother Peacock, about believing me. Please don't doubt the truth I am speaking right now.

"OK Dollygal, you're right I did say that, and I meant it. It just takes us a while to understand the way that you do. I believe you."

"It is kind of ridiculous for me to doubt what you are saying, considering everything we have gone through with Laszlo and Liaison.

"Tell me about Lily... who is she?" says Peacock.

"She came out of the mirror, and she says she is me! She speaks about a group called the Shadow Ones, and they live beyond the clouds." says Dollygal.

"That name sounds so familiar. Where is Lily?" says Peacock.

"She ran into the closet when she heard you come to the door." says Dollygal.

"Stand back and I will open the closet door and expose her presence." says Peacock.

"Aaaa haaa! ... come out of this closet at once and explain yourself... whomever you are." Peacock looks inside the closet.

"My strong manly power must have scared her and the Shadow Ones away...!!!"

Suddenly the mirror begins to tremble, and the room began to shake.

"What's happening here?" says Peacock.

"Step away from the mirror, brother Peacock." Dollygal screams.

"Do you think that she comes directly out of the mirror, Dollygal?" Peacock walks closer to the mirror.

He looks in the mirror and a shadow appear, and then Lily steps out of the mirror and stands in front of him. Peacock is stunned and cannot believe what is happening...

"I must be ... ... hallucinating or dreaming!" says Peacock.

"Hallucinating or dreaming?!" Ha... Ha... Ha..., I told you, Princess, they can't believe it. They do not have it in them. Look how quickly they forget." says Lily

"But you look exactly like Dollygal! Oh my...!!! I do not feel too good. I may be sick for a moment." Peacock falls to the ground.

Dollygal runs to help Peacock—

"Brother Peacock, wake up... wake up!

"Ha...Ha... look at the manly noblemen all passed out on the ground! He's supposed to be a great protector." Ha... Ha... Ha...

"Be quiet Lily. Where are your great Shadow Ones?" says Dollygal.

"My people are all around at all times." says Lily.

"The voice of the "Great Garden" is always all around. We can hear it and feel the great force that it brings. It is much greater than the Shadow Ones. It was the power and presence of the "Great Garden" that destroyed Laszlo." says Dollygal as she points her finger at Lily.

"Oh! You and your precious "Great Garden". The truth is Laszlo was weak. I'm different, I don't believe in the power of the Garden. Therefore, I feel nothing." says Lily.

The "Great Garden" is known to be connected, with everything in existence. I think that means you to Lily." says Dollygal.

"No way possible. I am opposite of you, so I am from the opposite power of you. Get it Princess."

"Maybe the opposite power is part of the "Great Garden". Get it, Lily." Dollygal speaks sarcastically.

Lily points her finger at Dollygal.

"You are trying to trick me, but it won't work."

"You are sent here to make me doubt. What if I'm with you, to make you believe?" says Dollygal.

"Believe what Princess?" asks Lily.

"Your connection to the "Great Garden"." says Dollygal.

"OK, just to humor you, Princess. Make me believe. Ha... Ha... Ha..." Lily stretches her arms out wide...

Chapter VI

THE ORIGINAL ORIGIN

P*eacock begins to slowly awaken.*

"Oh, I better go now. He might faint again if he sees me. Ha... Ha... Ha...

I will see you soon Princess!" Lily goes back into the mirror.

"I am all right Dollygal, where is she?" Peacock frantically looks around the room.

"She went back into the mirror, brother Peacock."

"OK, don't worry Dollygal, we will figure this out. We'll find out exactly what is happening. I promise." Peacock holds Dollygal in his arms.

In the meantime, Megan-spirit bear and Morgan-truth bear arrive from the tree village. Serpent carriage arrives bringing him up on the rickety-rockety road, leading to the huge double wood front door of the castle. They soon discover they're in-like minds.

"Mr. Serpent, we came to discuss an urgent and private matter with you and Mr. Peacock. It's about your sister Dollygal." says Morgan-truth bear.

"Of course, let's go inside and I will collect my brother so we can listen to what you have to say." says Serpent.

"Your home is as beautiful as I thought it would be. But are you in the middle of remodeling or something?" says Megan-spirit bear.

"Ahhh... we are in need of a little readjusting after an unexpected occurrence this morning." says Serpent.

"What kind of occurrence Mr. Serpent?" says Morgan-truth bear.

"I am quite sure you might be able to give some insight into what happened here this morning. A loud rumbling sound came rolling into our home; unearthing everything in its path, until it got to my little sister Dollygal."

"The rumbling sound and movement started in the village. We had never experienced anything like that before. But I do know that it is a new expansion opening in the Garden." Says Morgan-truth bear.

"What on the Earth could it be?! Is it here to destroy us?!" says Serpent.

"No Mr. Serpent, it is here to help all of us. We just don't know exactly how." says Megan-spirit bear.

"We do know that Dollygal is a part of the prophecy spoken by the ancestors of the village." says Morgan-truth bear.

"Wait... I will get Peacock so we can both hear about this. Please have a seat on the couch by the piano."

Serpent goes up the spiral staircase and down the hall leading to Dollygal bedroom. He opens the door and finds Peacock and Dollygal in a Tinder embrace.

"Is everything OK?" says Serpent.

"Brother Serpent the Shadow Ones are beyond the clouds and Lily is here to help them." Dollygal frantically waves her hands.

"Dollygal, please calm down. Let me explain to brother Serpent, what has happened in your room, OK?" Peacock speaks softly.

"The shadow people beyond the clouds?" May I ask who Lily is?" says Serpent.

"Lily is somehow the opposite of Dollygal, with a different agenda and outlook on things. She looks just like Dollygal!" says Peacock.

"Oh no... this can't be happening. Serpent shakes his head."

Please, brother Serpent, don't doubt any of this. It is all true, and it is happening. Dollygal caresses Serpent's face.

"I do believe it, little sister. Peacock, there is something I must tell you about. But first, we must go downstairs, Megan-spirit bear and Morgan-truth bear from the village are here with some urgent news." says Serpent.

"Whatever you have to say Serpent I'll accept it, and I forgive you."

"I forgive you too, my brother." says Serpent.

Dollygal, Peacock, and the Serpent hurry downstairs to greet Megan-spirit bear and Morgan-truth bear along with Godfrey, Professor Boo and Mr. Protege.

"Looks like the gang's all here. You guys are just in time to hear the urgent news from the village." says Peacock.

"The prophecy that we came here to share with you today is about Dollygal.

The ancestors of the village left a warning about a group called the Shadow Ones. According to the prophecy they live beyond the clouds.

There was a curse created by Ego, that would limit the minds of the people. The Ego one's survival depends on the lack of belief, that the people have in themselves." says Morgan-truth bear.

"That is what Lily said to me. She has three days, and she is waiting for everyone to doubt the Power of Love, me especially." says Dollygal.

"Dollygal is the one that holds the Power of Love; therefore being the one that can destroy the world they created. Liaison and Laszlo were sent here by the Shadow Ones and they were defeated by love." says Morgan-truth bear.

"I'm afraid I know all about the Shadow Ones. They were here at the time of Dollygals birth." says Godfrey.

"Godfrey, you knew about this, and did not say anything?! What do you mean they were here at Dollygals birth?" says Peacock.

"Please try to understand that this is the journey we are all on together. You're all on the path to making a great transition. It is not up to me to change anything. It is up to all of you to be the authentic true selves, that you were born to be. Be yourself!" says Godfrey.

"Be yourself, sounds like an exceptionally good title for your speech Mr. Peacock. To be your true self and speak your truth is obviously a mindset that destroys or transforms the Ego ones. That correlates with the curse placed upon the people and limiting their mindset. I think this is a legitimate prophecy." says Professor Boo.

"I agree completely Professor Boo. To be yourself means that you choose yourself." says Mr. Protege.

"Mr. Protege, my dear friend you have been an example of truth in my life. You have always been a truth teller, no matter what anyone else thought. That is authentically being yourself, my friend." says Professor Boo.

"So, the curse of the Shadow Ones is really about mind manipulation or trickery done to the people. In order to prevent them from becoming their true selves. says Mr. Protégé.

"Exactly, my friend." says professor Boo.

Serpent speaks with one eyebrow raised higher than the other,

"You explained that rather well Mr. protégé, I can clearly see how everyone is evolving tremendously. Peacock, I think I remember more about Mother and Father and the Shadow Ones. Remember that you have already forgiven me." says Serpent.

"Remember that you have forgiven me as well, my brother. Let us talk about this in the morning. Right now, we need to continue forward with the opening of the school."

"We will need to take each step forward with caution, as we have come this far, and we are almost there. We do not know our destination, but we are willing to go..."

Dollygal, Peacock, and the Serpent prepare for the school opening. Peacock and Serpent wearing classic suit attire which is matching with Dollgal's Red dress. The carriage is set saddled and ready to take them on a fascinating ride down the rickety-rockety road into the town, delivering them to the front doors of the "School of Intention".

Chapter VII

BE YOURSELF...CHOOSE YOURSELF

The town people of Lovely Ville all gather in their best clothes attire, for the long-awaited and highly anticipated opening night of the "School of Intention".

The aroma of food, fresh flowers, and perfumes on the ladies, permeates the air. White lights hang from the trees and align the streets, leading the people to the front door of the "School of Intention".

Dollygal, Peacock and the Serpent arrived in their carriage, and the people are delighted to see them.

The doors open to a brand-new redecorated school. The crowd of people quickly fills up the seats. Then Peacock stands at the podium to begin his opening speech by welcoming everyone.

"Thank you all, for coming this evening for the opening of the "School of Intention".

I thank my family and friends for their support.

We are deeply honored by your attendance and work ethic and for helping us put this whole celebration together.

The aroma of food is delightful, flowers, incense, fresh bread, pies, ham, etc... Ha... Ha... Haaaa!!!

We love to eat good food, here in Lovely Ville...

Without further ado... I would like to start off tonight by speaking from the heart...

What comes to me is... Bepeacelove!

We are now realizing that, we are the peace and the love. We have evolved to a state of mind that is beyond all-natural understanding.

In this space, we speak only about the greatness and positivity of one another.

Supporting and building confidence, instead of doubting our own abilities.

What may seem to be impossible... may we remember that...

Anything is possible... and nothing is impossible...!"

The people applauded loudly...

"Thank you... thank you... thank you very much...!"

I would like to talk about the new curriculum here at the "School of Intention". We are offering several classes designed to help everyone's transition into positivity and unity. This already has been accomplished with our tree village friends. We are expanding on a new higher level of consciousness. This is not complicated nor is it new stuff to learn. It is simply learning to be ourselves, trust ourselves, and choose ourselves.

We are equipped with everything that is needed in order to evolve to greater heights, to which we are expected to.

Lovelyville has experienced many challenges thanks to the "Great Garden" and my little sister—Dollygal.

We the people of Lovely Ville... are now aware of our own greatness! But we must know that there is much more work to do, and we will accomplish this by simply – being our true selves.

Peacock reads the curriculum:

Classes are scheduled as:

"Be yourself...Choose yourself."

Mr. Peacock

"Anything is possible...Nothing is Impossible."

Professor Boo

Mr. Protégé

"Conquering Ego." Mr. Serpent

"Believe." Mrs. Engirdle

"The Return to the Extraordinary"

Mr. Godfrey

The highlight of these classes is that it will aid in the manifestation of the new reality, that we are now experiencing here in Lovely Ville.

I would now like to turn over the podium to my brother Mr. Serpent.

The people applaud; welcoming Serpent to speak at the podium.

"Thank you all for your warm welcome and support. I am most honored to be able to speak on this most auspicious evening. As I look around, I see a village of united people. I remember the darkness and chaos of division, that once had us all consumed and literally separated us.

I stand here before you all and take responsibility for my part in it. I now realize that chaos and ignorance were surely a blissful state of mind for me. Separation and division were the only way I knew how to survive.

In this state of mind, lies become truth, and truth becomes lies. This mindset is not in alignment with our true selves. It has its own place woven between chaos and separation of the mind and from the source. I know now, that living in a survival mindset has limited properties. But living life from a different perspective opens doors to unfathomable, unimaginable, limitless possibilities...!"

Serpent point to Dollygal in the front row sitting with Mrs. Engirdle and Peacock.

"I would like to give thanks to my little sister Dollygal, for being the inspiration behind the classes I will be teaching.

She naturally embodies the spirit that conquers Ego. She has shown us the power of being a child and being very underestimated. She embraces and believes in this power, and she believes in herself. She is a true teacher by example, just like her Mother, once was.

Conquering Ego – is a class that will teach about letting go of things that limit our possibilities. It will also teach us how to embrace abilities we have not yet discovered. So, I hope this evening will bring some clarity to our vision for the future of Lovely Ville.

The townspeople of Lovelyville stood up applauded and cheered...

Then everyone gathered and enjoyed learning about all the other classes offered by Mrs. Engirdle, Professor Boo, Mr. Protégé, and Godfrey.

Their hopes for the future were exceedingly high, and they were filled with a new level of confidence.

They looked forward to the new challenges the "School of Intention" offered.

They celebrated till late night with good food, music, and insightful conversations.

Meanwhile, Dollygal had fallen into a deep sleep in her seat next to Mrs. Engirdle.

"Looks like Dollygal is tired." says Peacock as he picks her up from her seat.

"Professor Boo, Mr. Protégé, and I will stay here and close the school tonight. While you and Serpent take Dollygal home safely." says Godfrey.

"I will bring the carriage around to the front door." says Mr. Protege.

"Thank you, Godfrey, that is truly kind of you to offer your services. says Serpent.

"If you do not mind, I would like to stay and watch over Dollygal tonight, while you and Mr. Peacock get some sleep. You've both been working so hard at school and everything else." says Mrs. Engirdle.

"Thank you very much Mrs. Engirdle, of course you can stay. That would be of a great help to me and my brother." says Peacock.

The carriage rode home, which was brightly lit up by the shining moon. The dark night sky twinkled with shining stars.

The chili fresh air lightly blew across their faces as the carriage took them back down the rickety-rockety road leading to the castle in the "Great Garden".

Chapter VIII

"THE PROPHECY"

"Who comes the Angel..."

Who comes the Angel...
watching over me...
Watching over me...
Watching over me...

Who comes the Angel...
Praying over me...
Praying over me...
Praying over me...

Who comes the Angel...
Saying it Loves me...
saying it Loves me...
Saying it Loves me...

Who comes the Angel...
watching over me...
Praying over me...
Saying it Loves me...

Be the peace...Be the Love...

Be peace love...

M rs. Engirdle put Dollygal to bed. Then sat quietly in a comfy chair and watched her sleep. As she tosses and turns, a white light permeates and fills the room with a warm inviting presence. A voice emerges from the distance with a message...

"The happening is emerging everywhere. The rumbling sounds of the Earth is making itself heard throughout the "Great Garden".

It will no longer stay silent... the time has arrived for the great manifestation of the unknown and the unseen.

The happening is a blessing to many; yet a curse to a few. In order to live in balance and harmony with the "Great Garden", chaos must surrender or be conquered.

This prophecy has been honored by the ancestors of the tree people generation after generation.

Prophecy spoken by the ancestors from the past, present, and future. They foretold and brought forth the stories about certain ones born with pure hearts. Such ones would be able to live in the mundane world, yet be able to experience a higher vibrational understanding of the environment in which they live.

These pure-hearted ones will teach others by example. They will teach others to trust their hearts and believe in themselves, far greater than they could ever possibly imagine.

Such ones as this are born with the enlightened awareness of all great possibilities.

You, Dollygal, are one of these pure-hearted ones. You were born with the remembrance of the higher vibrational world that overlaps the mundane world.

The "Great Garden" is your birth home. It is the Alpha and the Omega, it is the Beginning and the End, it is the As Above; So Below, *yet, the manifestation of "The Happening," will reveal that there is no beginning or ending to the "Great Garden".*

The pure-hearted ones are made in the same likeness as the

"Great Garden". They live simultaneously in the past, present, and future. They can see and understand the known, the unknown, and the unseen.

Such ones as you Dollygal, are a blessing to many and a curse to a few. The prophecy speaks of the "Shadow Ones" that live beyond the clouds and has been watching the "Great Garden" and Lovely Ville.

They have watched your birth come forth from the divine love of your Mother and Father.

They have watched you be born through the womb of your great Mother.

Like you, she was born in the "Great Garden" and grew up in this Garden. She played in this Garden and discovered the magic, miracles, and presence of a mighty power that lives here!

The same teaching given to your Mother, is the same one for you at this auspicious time.

Do not doubt anything that you encounter from this point on.

It is all in your favor and nothing can prevent "The Happening"

The illusion that the "Shadow Ones" have created, has been dismantled. As above; So below is "The Great Happening".

It is the final merging coming into order within the "Great Garden".

It is moving through the Earth of the Garden and Lovely Ville, like thunder. The physical outcome of the manifestation of this roaring thunder, you have yet to know and to see.

When you awaken from this long sleep...

Remember all that has been given...

Then complete this journey and allow yourself to

connect and become like a bridge, as the manifestation

of the "Happening" arrives...!!!"

Mrs. Engirdle is shaken awake by rumbling sounds and movement in Dollygal room. The big chair slid closer to the bed. The mirror shook vigorously, then suddenly stopped as Dollygal awakened!

Dollygal stretches her arms over her head. Awww... is that you Mrs. Engirdle?"

"Yes... yes, it is me Dollygal. I stayed the night here to look after you until morning."

"I was dreaming that my bed shook me awake." Dollygal jokingly says.

"That was no dream, the rumbling movements of the Earth happened again." says Mrs.Engirdle.

"It is the "Happening" and it has arrived. It is the final merging of all order in the "Great Garden". Dollygal says as she excitedly jumps out of bed.

Then suddenly a long screen comes from within the mirror. The mirror explodes and shattered glass flies all over the room. Lily slowly emerges out of the wreckage.

Mercy Me!!! who is this standing before me Mrs. Engirdle's eyes open wide as she looks at Lily!

"This is Lily, Mrs. Engirdle, don't be afraid. She likes to make a grand entrance, as she arrives." Dollygal stands between Lily and Mrs.Engirdle.

"I can speak for myself Little Miss Princess. My name is Lily, and my people are the "Shadow Ones."

Dollygal, or shall I use your other name? Yeah, I think I like this one better!

Eve is lying to you about the "Happening". It is no such thing as that anymore. It will never take place" Lily speaks angrily.

The Shadow Ones have conquered the minds of the people and Lovely Ville. Right now, as I speak, their shadows are seen all over the sky and in your precious "Great Garden" Ha... Ha... Ha... Ha...!!!

"You are the liar... Lily. We have all come too far to start doubting our own experiences. Lovelyville, my brothers, and I have evolved to a greater understanding of the world that we live in. We have no need to doubt the blessings that we have already received."

As above; So below has taken place... Lily.

"The Shadow Ones" are the ones I believe. The prophecies are wrong, and the Shadow Ones are right. Your people can never believe in themselves – the way that the original prophecies speak."

Lily begins to walk around Mrs. Engirdle with hands behind her back.

"You see Mrs. Engirdle, special ones like Dollygal have an advantage on unfortunate ones like you. In fact, you want to know how special she is.

She can already figure this stuff out and know it is true, without really trying. I really hate that quality.

It just comes naturally for ones like her, and this kind of mindset. This type of power and belief system they're born with, that tells them they are better than everyone else around them.

Doesn't that make you feel like you're less worthy of such power?"

Lily angrily points her finger at Dollygal and says—

"Why are there ones, like her, walking around here embracing that type of power; that can destroy my people and our way of living?"

Mrs. Engirdle folds her arms together in front of herself.

"I've listened to you without any interruption. Now without any further ado, I would like you to listen.

Yes, Dollygal is an incredibly special one. In fact, she is so special that she uses her belief system, to help us realize the same belief system is given to us all.

She is here to help unfortunate ones like me, and help us to remember how extraordinary we really are!

If Dollygal was not born at this time, then people like Liaison and Laszlo would have succeeded in destroying us.

So, it looks like the prophecies handed down by the ancestors are correct!

My question now is who are you? Where did you come from? You're obviously the opposite of Dollygal, and a terribly angry and misguided little girl."

"I come from the mirror. That is my home. I was created in the likeness of the Shadow Ones by the Shadow Ones." says Lily

Dollygal pleads to Lily—

"Let me show you the "Great Garden" Lily. Let me help you see your likeness with it..."

"I don't want to be in any likeness with your precious Garden." says Lily.

"Well, you are whether you like it or not. You see Lily, in the "Great *Garden*", the opposite or the dark side is simply a part of oneself that is unaware of the power of its own light.

The "Great Garden" is where anything is possible, and nothing is impossible.

Unless you're afraid I might be right, and you will be wrong." says Dollygal.

"Of course, you think you've got the answers to everything. Let us go to the "Great Garden" Lily speaks sarcastically.

"No way, am I letting you both go unsupervised. I am going with you. I will leave a note for Mr. Peacock and Serpent on our way out." says Mrs. Engirdle as she wraps her cape around her shoulders.

"Dollygal here is a wrap for you to put on. It will be cold outside, this morning."

"Lily, I have one for you too, I'm sure Dollygal will not mind if you wear one of hers."

"I don't need one because I don't get cold." says Lily

"If that's the way you feel little girl, then no wrap for you." says Mrs. Engirdle

Meanwhile...

Peacock is awakened in his bed by the sounds of movement through the house. The creaky sound of the front door opening and closing left him suspicious. He gets out of his bed-adorned in gold bedding and slipped on his gold silk robe. Then he quietly went to the front room area of the house.

He looks around for anything unusual. Then he sees a note on top of the large black grand piano in the center of the room. He reads the note, then quickly gathers Serpent, Godfrey, Professor Boo and Mr. Protege.

"What is the emergency for waking up us all at this hour in the morning?" says Serpent.

Mrs. Engirdle left a note on the piano just a while ago, I will read it to you all. Peacock puts on his reading glasses—

"Dear Mr. Peacock and Serpent. Dollygal, Lily, and I have gone into the Garden. I cannot explain everything in this note. Lily has come from the mirror and the Shadow Ones. Dollygal will need your assistance."

We better all get dressed and find them in the Garden as soon as possible. The Shadow Ones will want to get Dollygal, since she is the biggest threat to the world they have created." says Godfrey.

"I guess this means no breakfast this morning." says Mr. Protege.

"We will eat along the way in the Garden. Those delicious new fruit trees will be perfectly ripe and full." says Professor Boo.

They all get dressed and leave through the back door. The morning dew drops trickle down from the vibrant trees, leaving a path leading them all into the most fascinating journey into the world of enlightenment.

Meanwhile Dollygal, Lily, and Mrs. Engirdle enter the vegetable and Rose Garden. Dollygal friends reach out to Lily, in the most peculiar way!

"Hey... Hey... Haaay...!!! Watch yourself before you hurt yourself." A sarcastic-sounding voice speaks out.

"Who said that? Are you trying to trick me, Princess?" Lily says to Dollygal with hands on her hips.

"What you heard Lily was Miss Anatolia. She lives in the vegetable garden with her family of leafy greens."

"Vegetables do not have the authority to speak. They are planted and then eaten by people." says Lily.

(Miss Anatolia's big leaves begin to shake rapidly)

"Authority!!! Oh, see you are cruising for a bruising... hmmm...

Kicking your way through our home, that way is obnoxious and rude behavior... hmmm...

Walking around here trying to look like Dollygal. You are an imposter!!!"

"It's my fault, Miss Anatolia. I should have told Lily about the "Great Garden" and all its inhabitants."

Lily, Miss Anatolia, and her sisters Miss Kale and Miss Romaine live in this area of the Garden. So, be mindful of how you walk through." Dollygal says to Lily.

"She saved you this time. But I know where you and those Shadow Ones come from." says Miss Anatolia.

"Oh great, now I need to be careful of some talking lettuce with an attitude!" Lily shakes her head.

"Did you call me a piece of lettuce?! No... no... I am a collared green... OK!

Watch yourself, before you hurt yourself." says Anatolia.

Mrs. Engirdle points ahead to the Rose Garden.

"Let us visit Miss Lottie down the way. Her pink petals are especially beautiful today."

"That is a great idea Mrs. Engirdle. Lily, I'll introduce you to Miss Lottie in the Rose Garden." says Dollygal.

"What is she – a talking rose?!" Lily sarcastically says.

"Yes, she and her family have been part of the Garden for a long time." says Dollygal.

"Oh, and what a beautiful big pink rose she is...

She is with her family of red roses, yellow roses, and white roses." says Mrs.Engirdle.

"I suppose we are going to have a conversation with Miss Lottie?" says Lily.

"Oh, indeed we are Lily. Miss Lottie loves meeting new people." says Mrs. Engirdle.

"Did I hear my name mentioned?" (Her petals flutter up and down, as she speaks in a Southern accent)

"Hello, Miss Dollygal and Mrs.Engirdle, it's so nice of you to come to visit.

Why... mercy... Mercy Me! Am I seeing two of you Miss Dollygal?!" Or have my eyes gone bad?!"

"No Miss Lottie, your eyes are OK. This is Lily, Mrs. Engirdle and I are showing her around the Garden. Lily has never been in a Garden like this before."

"But you and Miss Lily must be related somehow, right?"

Dollygal and Lily look at each other with confused looks on their face.

Mrs. Engirdle interjects—

"Of course, we told her all about you Miss Lottie." says Mrs. Engirdle.

"Her cheeks turn rosy, and red as she giggles..."

"You can believe everything you heard except for the potential budding romance between me and Mr. Godfrey. That man has kept me waiting for too long...!!!

I am quite sure he should have been pruning these trees by now. That is my chance to sweet-talk him for a while."

She giggles as her petals twirl up and down.

"OK, so enough about pretty me. I am saying this because if you don't stop me from talking girl...

I won't let you get one word in the conversation." she giggles.

"Now tell me all about yourself Miss Lily.

Where are you from?

What brings you here?"

"I'm from the mirror and I am here with my people, the Shadow Ones. This is the final chance to take what is ours and keep what is ours.

The Shadow Ones have already proven that people here in Lovely Ville cannot believe in themselves enough in order to become their true selves." Lily speaks with her hands on her hips.

"Miss Lottie moves close to Lily.

"Let me tell you something Miss Lily. It takes a lot of courage to believe in yourself. Especially when you're up against forces, which are constantly trying to confuse you. This "Great Garden" you are within right now is the place where all possibilities happen.

It might take a while, but eventually, it all falls into perfect order. Now you run along and let Dollygal show you more of this Garden."

Anatolia's voice is heard not far from the Rose Garden—

"I knew she was trouble from the moment I laid eyes on her... hmmm Shadow Ones! That just sounds like they up to no good!"

"Miss Anatolia always got a word or two to say. Do not pay her any attention, she speaks without thinking sometimes. She really does not mean any harm at all. Do you, Miss Anatolia?" Miss Lottie speaks loudly.

"I say what I mean, and I mean what I say... hmmm..."

"Well, maybe her words come out a bit strong. But it's just something you get used to over time." says Miss Lottie.

"No need to apologize for her rude behavior. What else would you expect from a collard green." says Lily.

Anatolia clears her voice and speaks—

"The same thing you would expect from someone traveling with shadows... Miss Lily. If that's your real name... hmmm..."

Dollygal interrupts the conversation—

"I think Miss Lottie is right, we should be moving along into the "Great Garden".

"Yes indeed, there is much more for you to see and learn Lily. The living waters, the waterfalls, the tree people, and much more." says Mrs. Engirdle.

"The living waters is just down the way, let's go, Lily." says Dollygal.

Chapter IX

ANYTHING IS POSSIBLE
NOTHING IS IMPOSSIBLE...

Dollygal, Lily, and Mrs. Engirdle continue the journey through the Garden.

Meanwhile, Peacock, Serpent, Godfrey, Professor Boo and Mr. Protege enter the Garden and are greeted by Anatolia and Miss Lottie.

"Oh, I see we are headed towards my favorite admirer in the Garden. Let me do the talking, she loves my smile." says Godfrey.

"Why my goodness, if it isn't Mr. Godfrey!" Miss Lottie giggles.

"Miss Lottie, it's always a pleasure seeing you my dear. I must say your petals are especially vibrant today."

Miss Lottie giggles as her petals twirsl up and down.

"Anatolia, how are you and your sister's Romaine and Kale?"

"We are doing fine Mr. Godfrey. Thanks to the classes we have had with Professor Boo and Mr. Protégé.

"Oh wonderful, we're so pleased that the classes are making a difference in your daily life." says Professor Boo.

"We are really looking forward to the other classes from the "School of Intention". I know it was a great success Mr. Peacock, Mr. Serpent.' says Anatolia.

"Yes, it was a very big success, and we hope everyone will benefit from the new classes." says Mr. Peacock.

"I don't mean to break up all this lovely chitter chatter, but we need to find Dollygal as soon as possible don't you think?" says Serpent.

"They just left from here. They could not be too much further ahead. Mrs. Engirdle and Dollygal were with Lily. She surely looked a lot like Dollygal!" says Miss Lottie.

They continued in a hurry through the "Great Garden" and then finally found Dollygal, Lily and Mrs. Engirdle by the lake of the "living waters".

"Aaaah...!!! What is that in the water?" says Lily.

"The living waters reflect your true self. That is, you Lily." says Mrs. Engirdle.

"Why do I look like that?"

"What is that behind me?"

"Those are your wings that you cannot see yet." says Mrs. Engirdle.

"I'm afraid of this place. Take me away from here." Lily hides behind Mrs. Engirdle.

"I thought you weren't afraid of anything Lily?!"

Looks like you're afraid to be yourself, Lily." says Dollygal.

"I am myself; the water is not telling the truth. It is trying to trick me and so are you Dollygal."

"I am not..."

"You are too."

"Please girls, I think I hear someone coming." says Mrs. Engirdle.

"Aaaah...!!! What is that coming out of the water?" Lily screams.

"Oh! Mystical! Mystical me! My sisters have come to play with me."

Seven sparkling silver balls of light float out of the living waters. The balls hover above the water. Then one-by-one, they burst open falling into the water making big splashes. One ball emerges from the waters, rapidly spinning in a circular motion. It stops in front of Dollygal, and transforms into one of the Seven Sisters! She gently touches her forehead against Dollygal's forehead.

Her name is Meridian. She wore a white dress shaped like a fluffy circle of foam. Her hair is golden sparkly and long to the ground. She has turquoise almond-shaped eyes that wink constantly. She has fish gills on each side of her face, that opens and closes frequently. The other sisters emerged from the waters as mermaids!

"Hello Dollygal, I am Meridian. We are from "The Kingdom Come", our world is deep within "The living waters"."

"You are my sisters that come to play, but you're different now. I don't think that we have ever met before." says Dollygal.

"No, we have not. I was born in our land, "The Kingdom Come". Because of the "Happening," we are now merged with the "Great Garden". As above, is now below. As above, so below.

"The other sisters belong to the waters now and they swim like fish with long beautiful tails." says Meridian.

"They are properly called mermaids. I met a beautiful mermaid when I was a young girl. I was with your mother, Dollygal. The mermaid swam right up to her, and they touched foreheads together." says Mrs. Engirdle.

"That is a special greeting from mermaids to ones who are in like minds with us." says Meridian.

"Look, someone is coming from across the Garden, and so are the Shadow Ones right behind them." Lily laughs while holding her stomach.

"Bother Peacock, Brother Serpent... the Shadow Ones are behind you. hurry... hurry...!"

Peacock, Serpent, Godfrey, Professor Boo and Mr. Protege arrived completely out of breath and rushes over to greet Dollygal and Mrs. Engirdle with great concerns and many questions.

"Oh, Brother Peacock, Brother Serpent, I'm so happy you're OK."

"We are happy to know you're okay Dollygal. We all were very worried about your safety." says Peacock.

"Mrs. Engirdle, we got the note you left. The Shadow Ones are making themselves known. We must continue to the Tree village, it's not far." says Godfrey.

"But wait, you must be introduced to Dollygal's new friend. Meridian is from the "living waters"." says Mrs. Engirdle.

"I thought Lily was the new look-alike friend." says Professor Boo.

"Wow, they do look alike. But they are quite different. That is good, you can learn from one another." says Mr. Protégé.

"No, Dollygal has nothing to learn from this problem child," Serpent speaks sarcastically.

"The Shadow Ones told me about you Mr. SsssSerpent!!!

Mr. Peacock, ask your brother if he has anything he wants to say to you and Dollygal." says Lily.

"I think I would rather meet Meridian." *says* Peacock.

Meridian steps forth and introduces herself. When she speaks, her voice echoes all through "The Great Garden".

"That is quite a name you have Meridian." says Peacock.

"I must say that you are quite enchanting." says Serpent.

Meridian looks at Godfrey and her eyes start to blink and her guilds flutter rapidly. Then she touches her forehead to his.

"She is from the land of "The Kingdom come"." says Godfrey.

"How did you know that?" says Peacock.

"Everything is happening as it should, Peacock. Let us go, we should be on our way to the Tree village." says Godfrey.

"Wait a minute everyone. What is that sound?" says Professor Boo.

"It's that same rumbling sound we heard back at the house." says Mr. Protege.

They all look at one another... "Ruuuuuun!!!!!"

They all ran quickly as the rumbling rattling sounds move through the Garden unearthing everything in his path. Meridian let out a loud screeching sound, before she jumps back into the rushing waters of the lake.

Peacock carries Dollygal, while Godfrey guides Mrs. Engirdle. Serpent reaches out for Lily's hand as they all try to outrun the rumbling rattling movement from the ground. But he missed her grip. They both stumbled and tumbled into "The living waters".

Twisting and turning under the water, Serpent reaches out his hand to Lily and she grabbed the hold. He pulls himself and her up out of the water. Then he is suddenly startled by his reflection in the water.

"Aaaah!!! Serpent is startled!"

"Forgive me, child, I should be tending to you. Are you okay?"

"I think I am okay." Lily coughs up water.

"I don't think you're okay, Mr. Serpent. Whom were those people standing next to you? I saw them in "The living waters"."

"No need to concern yourself with things that do not concern you." says Serpent.

"I saw your reflection too Lily."

"You did not SsssSerpent!"

"I would never have thought you to have wings like that." Serpent laughs.

"Okay, no time for chitter chatter. We must catch up to everyone at the Tree Village. I hear the rumbling sound coming back this way..."

Meanwhile:

Everyone made it to the tree village. Then realized that Serpent and Lily are left behind.

The village is shaken by the rumbling sounds of the Earth. They began to see Serpent and Lily running towards the village, along with the grounds splitting behind them at rapid speed!

Serpent and Lily made it into the village. Then they all watched the rumbling rattling movement of the Earth go towards the "Ever-flowing waterfalls".

Everyone embraces Serpent and Lily. While the people of the village are gathered at the waterfalls to chant, dance, and sing songs...

Dollygal jumps into Serpent's arms, and he swings her around in a circle...

"Brother Serpent, I'm so happy you made it."

"Aaaah... so am I, little sister. Besides, our brother Peacock would have sold all my classical music collection, if I had not made it." Serpent jokingly says.

"I certainly would have, brother of mine. Just like you would love to get your hands on the cigars Father left to me." Peacock laughs as he embraces Serpent with a strong hug.

"So, this is how the two of you express love for one another." says Lily.

"Yeah, it's a male ego dominance kind of thing, but it works for us. Peacock and Serpent laughs.

Everyone begins to laugh. Dollygal holds her stomach as her laughter gets carried by the wind and echoes throughout "The Great Garden".

Her laughter swooshes through the air with a vibrating glow. Stroking the trees, tickling the grass, and bursting into "The living waters".

Her laughter is greeted by her underwater sisters.

Meridian echoes a loud screeching sound with a vibrating glow. It swooshes up and out of the water, through the air, stroking the trees and tickling the grass...

"That is Meridian, she heard my laughter." says Dollygal.

"It seems like you both have a strong connection to one another. Maybe we will find out what that is all about. But for now, we better continue our way into the village." says Godfrey.

Chapter X

THE HAPPENING

B efore entering the Tree village, a strong gust of wind blows through "The Greats Garden".

The voice delivers a message, as it circles around at rapid speed.

"It... Is... Done..."

Meanwhile... back in the tree village, the sounds and the strength of the wind were felt, and the message was heard.

A small group of villagers led by Megan spirit bear and Morgan-truth bear; were following the wind as they were unexpectedly greeted by their friends!

They all embraced in a joyous reunion, and were very anxious to learn about the new transformations they were all experiencing in "The Great Garden".

"We are so happy to see you guys. We were on our way to the village; we really need help." says Peacock.

"We figured you would be needing help. This involves all of us. The great final transformation of "The Great Garden is taking place". says Morgan-truth bear.

"It is called "The Happening". The ancestors spoke about this, but generations of people lost belief in their teachings." says Megan-spirit bear.

"It seems like the destination of the voice and the rumbling Earth, is within "The ever-flowing waterfalls". We were all here and have seen the rumbling sounds that tear through the Earth, go directly into the waterfalls.

We all witnessed the wind and the voice message... "It is done", flow into the "Ever-Flowing Waterfalls"." says Professor Boo.

"Yes, we did. So, let's figure out what is the meaning and what it is all about." says Mrs. Engirdle.

"I'm sure the ancestors will have the answers about the flowing waters and the Shadow Ones." says Morgan-truth bear.

One of the tribe members with black hair and brown skin came forth; wearing beige animal skin pants and dark brown leather sandals with straps wrapping around his legs up to his knees. He wore a matching vest and carried a long stick.

"I will gather all the Engeo group to be there and listen to the message of the ancestors." He says to Morgan-truth bear.

"You will gather all the tribe people. They all plays a part in "The Happening".

We must not put hope in only certain groups. We must be united and allow the power of all groups to prevail. Regardless of your personal perceptions." says Megan-spirit bear.

"But the Engeo tribe is from the royal lineage of the king." The tribe member replies.

"Yes, and their message to us is to remember our power within the divine source." says Megan-spirit bear.

"You are correct Megan-spirit bear. We are all of one energy source of the highest vibration of the Universe. Now is the time to remember this truth. "The Happening" is about becoming one with this force." says Morgan-truth bear.

They all travel together into the tree village to begin ceremonies for the ancestors. So, they gather all the senior tribe people to assist and to bring clarity to the old ways.

Morgan-truth bear arranges for food, music, dance, and warm blankets for the sacred ceremony. A big fire was lit in a sacred area in the village.

The fire extended upwards into the sky. Creating a golden glow all around the trees and plants.

All the elders sat around the fire in a circle and held hands. Other villagers stood behind and joined in the prayer.

Morgan-truth bear guided Peacock, Serpent, Dollygal, and the rest of their group to sit in front of the fire, with the Elders.

Then Megan-spirit bear placed her hands together and began the ceremony with prayer and gratitude of Earth, Fire, Water, and Air.

She uttered the words repeatedly... As above; So below...

Then everyone began to repeat the words with her. Then suddenly the trees and plants began to shake, and twelve round balls of glowing white light, echoing a strange musical tune in a very deep baritone sound emerged forth.

Who is the body body... who's the body body... who's the body body... who's the body body... who's the body body...

Then the balls transform into twelve human figures of glowing luminous white lights.

They all speak in unison as they tell a story to the people—

"We are the ancestors and we have felt your hearts.

We are here because you are now ready for what is to come.

This is the time of the great happening.

This is a time that has been highly waited for by many.

Yet, highly unwanted by the Shadow Ones.

As this time names victory for all of you,

It means the destruction of their way of life.

Please... do not have heaviness on your hearts.

They have used manipulation and trickery to steal what has been rightfully yours, from the very beginning of time.

Make no mistake, the Shadow Ones know how great the power is, that you hold within!

Their way of survival was to create a new world, that is like the angelic realms. But they put themselves in charge as hierarchy.

The trickery was a smooth transition orchestrated by the Shadow Ones.

They taught the people to rely on something other than "The Great Garden".

The Shadow Ones taught people to rely on the world they had created.

According to them, you work hard and achieve success at any cost.

They taught separation to the people, in order to show that some are more superior, and some were not.

As the people were taught to utilize all these tools of thought, they never realized that they did not speak of "The Great Garden" anymore!

Each generation of people taught the children about these survival tools; but none taught the children about "The Great Garden".

They became satisfied with just knowing how to survive. They had no desire in wanting to know how to live!

Because all have been forgotten.

Because it is now all just a fable, that some old men spoke about long, long ago.

For this reason, such ones are born to remind you of what you have forgotten.

They act as a bridge from this physical world of existence, to "The world of all possibilities"

Such ones have the ability to remember a Divine purpose for everything.

Such ones are spoken of in the prophecies.

Such ones as this..., are always hunted by the hunters!

Envied by other forces and ostracized by other groups that do not understand them.

They remember "The Great Garden" and "The Great Garden" remembers them.

Such a one sits with us in the circle. Yet another one sits in this circle, unaware of their humble beginnings and their earthly family. This one represents the opposite of the other and the awareness of what is temporary in this world. There is a story waiting to be told, and it will be finished by us..."

Serpent stands up and speaks to the circle of friends—

"I have a story to tell, and let it be finished by the ancestors.

On the night of my little sister's birth was also the death of our parents. I insisted on being with Mother, but Father disagreed because he knew they were using me to get to Mother.

They told me that there were two babies to be born. One was to be given to them, and one was to be destroyed.

I was chosen by them to carry out this plan. In return, I would get power over Lovely Ville and "The Great Garden".

At the time, I was in a very deranged state of confusion. I felt alienated and distant from my Father and my brother Peacock. The Shadow Ones visited me often when I was a kid, playing in the garden. They made me feel important, but now I know they were feeding my Ego so they could use me to carry out their purpose against my own family. As a kid, they led me to believe that I was the special one.

But Mother told me that I was not the one that they were seeking. She always told me that I was special to her, but it was not enough for me. She and my Father knew about the Shadow Ones, and how they were seeking to get my little sister at her birth. Father figured out my part in the plot, so he ordered Peacock to protect our mother from the Shadow Ones as he assisted with the birth.

Father placed Mother in the carriage to hide. But the Shadow Ones supernatural presence startled the horses. They went running out of the castle gates in the pouring rain, with Mother and Father in it.

The Shadow Ones detained Peacock and allowed me to go after them and carry out the mission.

When I arrived at the carriage, it was wrecked off the road. I heard a baby crying, so I rushed over to the carriage and there was my Mother holding a baby in one arm and my Father in the other arm. He delivered the baby before he died. I have never seen my Mother look so weak and broken.

But then she suddenly started to prepare herself for another birth that was unexpected. I assisted with the birth of the second child. I also watched my Mother pass away slowly afterward. In her last breath, she pleaded with me to do the right thing with the babies.

I knew I would have to answer to the Shadow Ones. So, I left one baby under the Sycamore tree, and took the other baby with the intention of giving it to them.

But when I got there with the baby, they told me it was the wrong one. I needed to bring the other one instead.

I pleaded to them but somehow there was a difference between the babies, according to them. I left the baby with them and went to get the other one.

When I got back to the carriage, I reached for the firstborn baby underneath the Sycamore tree. She started to cry, and I held her and talked about our great Mother and Father. I surprisingly felt a connection and warm feeling inside myself.

Then the Sycamore tree spoke to me and said that I have love within me, and the child would love me as my parents did.

I knew I could not give the baby to the Shadow Ones. I wrapped her up and decided to find my brother Peacock. But then he showed up and demanded that I hand him the child.

He said that he would not let me get away with killing our parents, stealing our sibling and destroying our family legacy. He swore to never let me anywhere near our little sister. He was only trying to protect her, and he was right to do so.

We were terrible enemies from that point on. Then our little sister reunited us by winning a simple little game.

I never told anyone about the other child, because when I did get a chance to go back, it was gone and so were the Shadow Ones.

The Sycamore tree told me that the Shadow Ones had taken the child. I now believe that child is Lily." says the Serpent.

The Serpent covers his face with his hands—

"Please brother of mine, say you can forgive me."

"It is already forgiven, brother of mine. I can feel that you have forgiven me as well." says Peacock, as he hugs the Serpent.

Then as Dollygal and Lily join Peacock and Serpent in a big healing embrace; a big glowing circle of light emerges from the Earth underneath and circle around them.

The strong force lifts them up into the air, spinning and magically weaving them together. Then gently releasing them back to the ground.

Then the ancestors speak a message from beyond—

"The greatest healing; is about total forgiveness.

Your family has been reunited to its fullest capacity.

Because of this reunion, the door to "All great possibilities" is now open to all people.

They will be able to remember what they have forgotten!

The two children were conceived at two different times.

The Shadow Ones captured your Mother and when she returned home, she was impregnated with a child. She never knew until the birth in the carriage.

They planned on gaining control over "The Great Garden" by utilizing the power of the chosen one, that has the power to eventually destroy their way of life. Yet, the world of illusion they created was not to ever come into existence. They were rebellious against their natural home, which was — "The Great Garden".

The negative thoughts stemming from envy and jealousy, and whom should have absolute power created a force field of energy; that eventually separated them from the divine source from which they had come.

They knew their world is made up of misinformation and thoughts that were opposite of the truth, we're only temporary. The only way to make the illusion (which is the unreal made real) solid and permanent, was to take the original and the only true power of overall creation which resides in "The Great Garden".

To believe and accept the illusion created by the Shadow Ones...

Is to believe and accept your own limitations, which you become a victim and supporter of the illusion made through manifest.

To set your intentions on directly misguiding others and hope to steal, kill and destroy the light from within; is the delusional mind of the perpetrator.

This world brought forth by the perpetrator is only manifested by the ones that have little belief in their true selves.

The Shadow Ones has only had power over the people's inability to believe, that they are far greater than they could ever possibly imagine.

The only way the Shadow Ones gained power is because of the people's inability to believe in themselves.

The power from within; can never be taken away,

It can only be given away.

Suddenly the ancestors began to slowly disappear into The Dark Night. Slowly they all turned into white specks of fire floating lights, that moved rapidly around the crowd of villagers, then dispersing in great light into the sky!

Then suddenly the trees began to bend and shake rapidly as the thrust of wind blew viciously.

Everyone held on to one another as they were nearly blown out of the area.

Then as the wind subsided and the trees no longer shook, everyone sat quietly waiting for the next Happening.

Then a large dark shadow appeared. Seemingly taking over the sky and acting as a blanket covering up the shining stars.

Then three shadow figures emerged from this darkness and were illuminated by the firelight.

They stood side-by-side, with the tallest one in the middle. They spoke in unison and sounded like any other man, and their presence felt strong and very heavy upon everyone in the circle.

They told a story about the birth in the Garden—

We took what was rightfully ours, one child made in our likeness and the other child made in the likeness of "The Great Garden".

One would fulfil its duty to protect the new world created by us;

The other would fulfill its duty to bring forth eternal knowledge and divine awareness.

One child could help in the creation of our kind; while one could assist in the destruction of our kind.

For an exceptionally long time, we have gained our strength and power from the people.

The uncertainty and the inability to believe in the power that is held within you,

Is our life force to this world we have created out of our newfound likeness.

But now, we have felt an undeniable change—we are weaker than ever before!

The resistance to the divine order within "The Great Garden" is no longer relevant.

Nor is our final plan of taking over "The Great Garden," possible.

The prophecy of separation is being fulfilled, but not in our honor.

Not in the way that we hoped...

Not in the way that we spoke...

Seemingly our words and our thoughts have been turned in the opposite direction.

Our intentions no longer have the power of persuasion of speaking the opposite of Truth.

Yet, now the Truth brings forth the understanding of order from which opposite was born.

Because of this, our intentions have failed to manifest.

Because of this, Truth of the opposite is now being heard from "The Great Garden".

The prophecy has been fulfilled by the people within "The Great Garden," and Lovely Ville.

We have allowed the best of our kind to fulfill this prophecy to our advantage, but Liaison, Laszlo, and now Lily, we're all overcome by "The Great Garden".

We have no other choice but to return to our humble beginnings within "The Great Garden".

The tree village people began to dance and cheer loudly.

Then Lily stepped in front of the Shadow Ones and interrupted the villager's celebration.

She held the palm of her right hand out towards the villagers, and the left hand on her hip as she spoke—

"Wait... I think we should thank them, rather than celebrate their defeat. They are resistors of the light, and so was I until now; and so were all of you!

I was taught to be the opposite of the truth and now I am being taught the truth about the opposite.

I came here out of loyalty to the Shadow Ones. I came here as their final tool to destroy belief in the enlightenment everyone had rightfully received.

I planned to do this by casting doubt on what you had already experienced. Then I was going to manipulate you into doubting your own experience.

Yet, I am the one who began to doubt my own connection to the Shadow Ones.

I believe the word was spoken by the great ancestors. I believe the Serpent spoke the truth about the birth of my sister Dollygal and me.

I believe the Shadow Ones are defeated, because I have felt what I have always been taught against—which is love and unity.

I believe everyone here has something to learn from the Shadow Ones. Everyone has been a resistor of the light within themselves.

Therefore, the Shadow Ones are a part of us all! A part that we could easily become due to the lack of courage, to allow ourselves to become something far greater than we could possibly imagine.

Lily turns around to look at the Shadow Ones—

The wind began to blow viciously, and the trees and plants began to bend and shake rapidly...

The dark shadow hovering over the sky and in front of the sparkling stars, suddenly began to move swiftly in a circular motion and was pulled down into the Earth...

Then released; as it bursts upwards into white, blue, and purple light into the sky and leaving a streak of its sparkly dust, connecting from Earth to the Sky...

Then the loud rumbling sounds returned and began lifting the ground rapidly moving through the trees and bushes. Then headed in the direction of the holy circle taking place with everyone, then going around them and down into the "Forever flowing waterfalls" nearby.

The waves in the water shook viciously then simply and softly subsided into calmness. The white waterfall seemingly fell from the sky into the lake of water below. The sound was quiet and soft as the waves gently flapped together against rocks in the water...

The gold and silver Frollie lollie people came to the top of the water making a rare appearance for all to see.

Then vividly appearing on each side of the waterfalls, (looking out for any thoughts of doubt) stood four white angelic protectors from the North, South, East, and West.

Their golden wings expanded as high into the sky as the "Forever flowing waterfalls".

Then a deep baritone-sounding voice spoke, and its message echoed throughout the Garden.

BELIEVE!!!

Then the sounds of roaring thunder were heard and the rumbling sounds under the ground swiftly moved through "The Great Garden" and Lovely Ville...

The "Forever-flowing waterfalls" split wide open, revealing and bringing forth an enormous mountain that seemingly had no beginning or end!

The fiery heat of the mountain is in perfect union with the living waters.

The top was above in the sky and the bottom was somewhere within the water below...

At the bottom of the mountain, a manifesting pathway leading slightly upwards becomes visible. Shimmering gold dust softly shifts itself into place on the ground, while quiet footsteps form gently and miraculously...

Chapter XI

AS ABOVE...SO BELOW...

The circle of villagers was humble and incredibly grateful for the insightful truth of the prophecies that were handed down generation after generation.

No longer did they have unanswered questions...

No longer did they worry about the legitimacy of the prophecies...

No longer did they doubt the storytelling, that the elders within the village told them...

No longer did they doubt that "Anything is possible... and Nothing is Impossible..."

The circle of villagers began dispersing slowly, as Megan-spirit bear and Morgan-truth bear began to lead everyone back to the town and the village...

As they arrived, they felt something new, and they witnessed something new.

A new language was developing between the elders and the younger and new generation.

Standing side-by-side and hand-in-hand,

they released the final stage of the illusion of separation.

The elders all spoke together—

"We let go of what separates us..."

"We embrace what connects us..."

Spoken by the youths—

"We let go of what we thought to be old and untrue..."

"We recognize, believe, and respect the messages from the old into the new, are one and the same."

"We also accept your way of expression is different from ours, yet it is just as powerful." says the elders.

We have forgotten the prophecies about Earth Mother and Father Sky. It talks about many children they have and the different "Gifts" that all their children received.

These gifts were to be used to keep the universal order. Each group of children that were born, filled up every continent on the planet, and each were given apart of the secret code.

Together, they hold the combination code of life that unifies them with the planet. But if they are separated, then the code is incomplete and can be stolen and misused in order to conquer the planet.

These children were especially important and incredibly special because of what was within them. A different part of the sacred code of life is given to each of them. They were all a part of a divine plan to maintain order. Therefore, the community is especially important to Earth Mother and *Father* Sky.

Morgan-truth bear then approaches and intervenes with the elders and the youth groups.

"We stood here and listened to all of you. We were overwhelmed by the true connection you all displayed. You have found common ground where you are equal in power, and your likenesses are now your biggest strengths. The seeds of brotherhood, sisterhood, and familyhood have fully developed." Morgan-truth bear holds his arms out and embraces everyone.

Megan-spirit bear comforts Dollygal, Peacock, Serpent and friends—

"We are having an insightful journey together and I am sure it is not over yet. But we are all very tired and need food and shelter. We will prepare a space for all of you. Please come with me and our people. We will show you the way to all accommodations."

The tree village celebrated the unknown arrival of something new, with a full night of good food, music, and dancing.

Then a night of heavy rest fell upon them. Rain poured down in the village, the Garden and Lovely Ville.

The magical soft Dewey drops of rain, pitter-patter against the trees, bushes, flowers, plants, grass, and all other unknown parts of "The Great Garden".

Lovelyville is overwhelmed by the wind accompanying the rain as it seemingly creates an unknown musical tune, with every raindrop that hits the buildings, gravel streets, doors, and rooftops.

And the clop pity clop sounds from the horse's feet delivered the base sounds connecting rhythm!

The unique splashing sounds from different shoes and boots on the feet of the people, as they run to shelter themselves, collaborate masterfully together; creating a tiptoe tap-dance on the gravel streets.

The dance of the raindrops accompanied by the wind continued down the gravel streets, across the rooftops and doors; and softly trickling down the sides of buildings and reentering the flowing waters leading back to "The Great Garden" in all its inhabitants.

As the morning drew near, the rain was misty, calming, and quiet. Powerful rays of the Sun began drying the dampness of the Earth.

Birds were chirping...

The squirrels were gathering...

The animals and all creatures of the land were impatiently stirring around the tree village...

Then an unknown tune of a new presence was heard and it awakened everyone...

Professor Boo and Mr. Protégé, awaken simultaneously in their room.

"Professor boo, did you hear that sound?"

"Yes, I heard that sound, but it's not like the one we heard before."

Peacock and Serpent, frantically burst through the bedroom door.

"Have either of you seen Dollygal, Mrs. Engirdle, or Lily?" says Peacock.

"Not at all. Where do you think they could have gone?" says Professor Boo.

"At this point, anything is possible, and nothing is impossible." says Serpent.

"You're sounding more like your little sister each and every day Serpent!" says Peacock.

"Yeah, and I will take that as a compliment." says Serpent.

"Did you hear the sound?" says Mr. Protégé.

"How could we not hear it!" says Peacock.

"Oh, on the contrary, my friends. That was more like a big deep voice seemingly heard everywhere." says Serpent.

"This sounds like something connected to Dollygal." says Professor Boo.

"Let us go and find Godfrey, he went out for a walk in the rain early this morning. Let's find them before anything else happens." says Peacock.

They all walk outside and find Godfrey looking in the direction of "The Grand Mountain" as if in a trance, with his hands comfortably folded behind his back.

"Hey, Godfrey, where have you been?

Dollygal, Lily, and Mrs. Engirdle are missing again." says Peacock.

"They're not missing at all my friends."

"If they're not missing, then where are they, Godfrey?" says Peacock.

"What are you looking at?" says Serpent.

"It is called "The Grand Mountain". Close your eyes, then open them again and you'll see."

"What do my eyes see before me? I have heard many tales and prophecies speaking of this, but I never believed it to be true." says Professor Boo, as he stands next to Godfrey.

"At this moment, Dollygal would tell me not to doubt anything, so I won't. How did we miss seeing this, Mountain?!"

It is enormous, it's too big to miss." says Peacock.

"You can say that again Mr. Peacock. Wow! It's everywhere! Ha... Ha... Haaaaa...!!!

"Where did it come from?" Mr. Protege jumps around excitedly.

"It's time to see it. This is all part of the journey, my friends. Dollygal is taking Lily and Mrs. Engirdle to the mountain." says Godfrey.

"Okay, now a logical question would be – why is she taking them there?"

But we are not going to get an answer to that, are we?!" The Serpent spoke sarcastically.

"No." says Godfrey.

"Ha... Ha... I could have told you that Mr. Serpent." says Mr. Protege.

Megan-spirit bear, Morgan-truth bear quickly approached the others as they ran from within the village. Completely out of breath, they stand looking at the mountain in amazement!

Godfrey stands between them and puts his hands on each of their shoulders.

"The Earth Mother told Megan-spirit bear and me about this mountain when we were kids. It turned into an old prophecy spoken by the king in our village." says Morgan-truth bear.

Megan-spirit bear interrupts—

"The king is missing from his room. I think Dollygal is missing too."

They're not missing my friends. But yes, Mrs. Engirdle and Lily and perhaps the King are with Dollygal." says Godfrey.

"We are all ready for the continuation of our journey together.

As we make our way, let us remember to say, thank you!" says Megan-spirit bear.

They journey down one path that led them out of the village and towards the mountain. The closer they got to the foot of the mountain, the voices and their message became clear to everyone.

"Who's the body body... a deep voice speaks.

"I got it. The voice is saying... who's the body body." says Mr. Protégé.

"Yes, but what does that mean?" says Professor Boo.

"Well, it seems our little sister would know the answer to this one too. Perhaps the voice is a friend of hers!" Serpent speaks sarcastically.

"I think your right Serpent. She would be able to understand what the voice message is saying. It is probably a friend of hers, due to a deep connection they share." says Peacock.

"It's time for us to understand the voice message." says Godfrey.

"We are almost there; I can see the bottom of the mountain." says Morgan-truth bear.

The voice sang louder—

Who's the body body... Who's the body body...

who's the body body...

Suddenly everyone falls to their knees, as they become overwhelmed by the message.

Who's the body body... I the body body

Who's the body body... you the body body

Who's the body body... he the body body

Who's the body body... she the body body

Who's the body body... we the body body

Aaaaahhhh!!!

Chapter XII

BE YOURSELF. LET YOURSELF BE, YOUR TRUE SELF

A New Tree...

A new tree has blossemed and sprung forth in "The Great Garden."

It stands next to the most magnificant tree in the Garden...

It is called the tree of doubt. Its a bare branched tree, that can only grow a new leaf by awknowleging its likeness to the Garden.

A song was given to the tree by the Earth Mother
and those who believe, can hear it sing...

Heaven is a place in my my mind...

Heaven is a place in my body...

Heaven is a place in my spirit...

Heaven is a place I believe in...

Heaven is a place on Earth...

Meanwhile, up ahead Dollygal has arrived and is standing with the King, Mrs. Engirdle and Lily, at the bottom of the mountain where the Earth comes together with "The flowing waters".

Lily joyously jumps up and down splashing in the water, as she points to the sky—

"Look... Look at the streaks of red over there!"

"That's a rainbow for me. I see orange now." says Dollygal.

"I can see yellow forming brightly." says the King.

"Green, blue, indigo, and Violet." says Mrs. Engirdle, as she sits on a big rock.

"Please Dollygal, come sit on my lap dear child. I want to thank you so much."

"You want to know the biggest thing I am thanking you for child... Eve?"

"What is that Mrs. Engirdle." says Dollygal.

"One of the hardest things for people to do is to be themselves. Thank you for being your true self all the time... Eve." says Mrs. Engirdle as she gives Dollygal a big hug.

"I don't mean to interrupt such a tender moment but, I must say that I absolutely concur with everything you've just spoken to Miss Young Eve." says the King, as he kneels on one knee and kisses Dollygals right hand.

Dollygal giggles and holds her belly with her left hand as the King continues to talk.

"I had a dream about you. It showed you escorting me to my next destination. This brave, bright-eyed little girl allowed herself to "Awaken" to a true "Gift," and what did you do with it? You taught us all, that we have a "Gift" as well. Ha... Ha..."

"When I ordained you, Queen of the tree village – I redeemed my people and myself. Now I see you are the Queen of the entire Garden!"

"Now I agree with everything you've just spoken." says Mrs. Engirdle.

"Hey, someone is coming." Lily yells.

"It's Peacock, Serpent, Godfrey, Professor Boo, and Mr. Protege." Dollygal yells joyfully.

"Is that Morgan-truth bear carrying Megan-spirit bear?!" says the King.

"Yes, she must have fallen ill." says Mrs. Engirdle.

Peacock and Serpent call out to Dollygal, as they run to greet her with a big hug.

"Dollygal, are you all right?" says Peacock.

"Yes, I'm fine brother Peacock."

"Lily, how are you?" says Peacock.

"I'm on a wild and fascinating journey with my sister Dollygal, and I'm OK." says Lily.

"It is starting to feel more appropriate to call you Eve. I think it has something to do with this mountain. Just like the song we heard along the way here." says Serpent.

"That is the voice of the mountain, brother Serpent." says Dollygal.

Morgan-truth bear lays Megan-spirit bear by the water and gently splashes it on her face.

"Megan-spirit bear... wake up!"

"What happened? Where are we?" says Megan-spirit bear.

"We are finally at our destination." says Godfrey.

"Hi Megan-spirit bear, a message is given to you. Are you ready to hear it?" says Dollygal.

"Yes Dollygal, I am." Megan-spirit bear says with a smile.

"You have a gift coming to you Megan-spirit bear. It is a set of wings just for you." Dolygal says with a big smile.

"Oh my...!!! What will I do with them?" says Megan-spirit bear.

"Hey, I'm sure you will know soon." says Morgan-truth bear.

"There is a message for you to Morgan-truth bear." says Dollygal.

"What is it?"

"Your gift is a crown aligning you in unity with nature." says Dollygal.

"Thank you Dollygal, I will fully embrace this new gift." says Morgan-truth bear.

"I'm so tired I can hardly keep my eyes open. I need to rest a moment." Megan-spirit bear falls into a deep sleep.

Then the golden manifested pathway begins to shimmer and glimmer. The dirt shifts itself around, then slowly lifts upward and forms itself into two familiar physical figures clothed in long white robes.

They come forth and greet everyone. Peacock and Serpent step forward with Dollygal, as they look on in amazement.

"Mother?!" says Serpent.

"Father?!" says Peacock.

"Mom... dad?!" says Dollygal.

"Yes, children of mine, it is your Mother and Father.

We are here to assist our daughter – Eve. This joyful baby was born and held in my arms for a short amount of time.

So, bubbly and so beautiful that the name Dollygal came forth from me. I knew this child emersed with hope, faith, and charity had arrived." says the Mother as she hugs Dollygal.

The Father steps forward and takes Dollygal by the hand—

"Dollygal come here, and let me hold my special daughter. I want you to know that we will always be with you, and will support you in everything that you will do.

Remember, that "The Great Garden" is forever manifesting itself into the highest level of greatness and ultimate perfection, for the greater good of all.

I leave you with these words—

"Anything is Possible, and Nothing is Impossible" "As above; so below"

"My sons, please step forward and greet your Father."

He puts his right hand on Peacock's left shoulder, and his left hand on Serpents right shoulder as they stood before him.

"I'm immensely proud of you both. You have got great and many things to do. The people of Lovely Ville are in great hands and so is Dollygal." The father says with a smile on his face.

The mother intervenes and steps forward in front of the Serpent—

"There is no reason to feel this way, my son. Yes, you have already been forgiven.

Everything done out of strife or malice is transformed and used for the greater good.

I love you – my son Serpent; and I love you – my son Peacock, and our other daughter and your other sister – Lily.

"It's time for us to go now. Lily, come with us." says the father as he holds the Mother's hand.

"It's time to go Mrs. Engirdle, Mr. King, and Godfrey." says Dollygal.

Lily engages in a handshake and hug with Dollygal—

"Ya know Dollygal, I'd like to claim you the winner.

You never doubted yourself or the truth, within the three days. You exposed and seemingly destroyed my family the "Shadow Ones". But you really helped us to transform into our true original selves.

I am truly grateful for your head being in the clouds and Earth. simultaneously. I guess my new brothers aren't too bad after all!

They're both quite brave and love you very much." says Lily.

"They love you too Lily." says Dollygal.

"Yeah, I can believe that because I believe in you, my sister. Hey, and whatever it is that you are doing, I have no doubts about it, at all," says Lily as they hold hands.

"Thanks, Lily. Hey, you're glowing." says Dollygal.

"Hey, I'm vibrating like you sister." Lily twirls around and then point at Dollygal.

"You are vibrating like me?!"

"You are vibrating like me!" says Dollygal, as she twirls around.

"I guess our likenesses are showing." says Dollygal as they giggled together.

"Looks like our brothers are going to have a difficult time with this transition." Says Lily as she puts her arm on Dollygal's shoulder.

"Where is everyone going?" Peacock looks at everyone in confusion.

Godfrey embraces Peacock and the Serpent with an endearing hug.

"My journey with you has come to an end. But we continue together through the heart. We have done great work during this journey and because of it, "As above; So below" is now complete." says Godfrey

"Well, what about Dollygal? What is happening? What is she to do? We need her here with us." Peacock covers his face with his hands.

"Brother of mine, we must support her in whatever she has to do." Serpent embraces his brother.

Professor Boo approaches Godfrey—

"I sensed that something more was going on with you, my friend. But I could have never imagined it would be this. It has been an honor and a privilege to work with you, Sir Godfrey. You have been a very instrumental component in this journey together; thank you, Sir." says Professor Boo, as he shakes Godfreys hand.

"It has been a pleasure Mr. Godfrey, and I'm going to miss you very much." Mr. Protege begins to cry as he hugs Godfrey.

"No, you won't miss me at all Mr. Protege."

"Oh, I'm quite sure I will Mr. Godfrey Sir."

"Ha... Ha... You'll all see enough, my friends."

Then suddenly a deep sleep fell upon Peacock, Serpent, Professor Boo, Mr. Protege, Megan-spirit bear and Morgan-truth bear, and the entire Garden.

Then the final awakening was accepted, and the word became flesh.

Sparkling like a diamond in a bright yellow tulip style dress and matching socks, Dollygal gently touches Peacock and Serpent on the forehead with her finger.

Then watching them slowly begin to wake up.

As they lay on the floor looking upwards, the reflection of the Sun intertwines itself with Dollygal.

"Dollygal, is that you?" says Peacock, as he put a hand up to block the sunlight.

"I think our little sister travels with the Sun now."

Serpent jokingly speaks as he puts his hand up to block the sunlight.

"Dollygal, we are so happy to have you back with us. I thought we'd never see you again." Peacock and Serpent embrace Dollygal.

"So, what was it like? Where are Mother and Father and everyone?" Serpent and Peacock spoke together.

"Please don't ask questions like that, you guys."

Serpent's left eyebrow raises higher than the other. Then engages in a confused glare with Peacock.

"From the look on your face... I can clearly see that you were expecting much more of an answer than that... hmmmmm..."

"OK, maybe a little bit. We can get back to this later." says Peacock.

"Hey, wake up everybody. She's back. Dollygal is back." says Mr. Protégé.

"Indeed, you have made your way back. What a powerful journey you have accomplished Miss Eve."

"Oh, it is OK for me to refer to you as Miss Eve?" says Professor Boo.

"That's OK with me Professor Boo. I'm very happy to see you all again.

Morgan-truth bear, are you all, right?"

"Yes, I'm fine Dollygal. I'm so pleased that your journey brought you back to us. Just in time to help find Megan-spirit bear. I don't see her anywhere."

"Here I am. I'm trying out my new wings!"

Everyone watches as Megan-spirit bear flies down from the top of a tall tree with her new green, gold, and blue wings!

"Megan-spirit bear, you can fly!!! Well, I guess it shouldn't be such a surprise Ha... Ha..." says Morgan-truth bear.

"What is that on your head, Morgan-truth bear? It looks like a crown. Perhaps part of a crown on your head." says Megan-spirit bear.

Megan-spirit bear has blue, green, and yellow wings and can fly like a fairy. Morgan-truth bear has part of a gold crown on his head. The rest of it comes later, as he continues his transformation.

Chapter XIII

ALL IS LOVE...

"The laughter that guided us..."

The laughter that guided us, was inside us all...
We all knew the same direction...
We all knew and heard the call...
We all knew the way to the great mountain and the waterfalls...

*D*ollygal *speaks to Megan-spirit bear and Morgan-truth bear. Her big oval-shaped eyes sparkle with glittery lights as she speaks—*

"The King has passed on his crown to you Morgan-truth bear, and along with it comes great responsibility. You and Megan-spirit bear have another great initiation.

You will continue to lead the Tree Village as the King. The completion of your crown will take place along the way.

Megan-spirit bear, you have been chosen as the Head Fairy of the tree village. You will continue to lead with Morgan-truth bear.

Your internal connection with Earth Mother will allow you to understand nature.

"The Great Garden" will work with you, and you will know and understand the language of the trees, grass, flowers birds; as I do."

Megan-spirit bear and Morgan-truth bear kneel on one knee as they speak to Dollygal—

"We have a lot of good work to do, and we are very honored to be a part of something this beautiful. Thank you Dollygal, for simply being yourself.

That is the universal understanding of our initiations that has taken place." says Morgan-truth bear..

"Exactly, that is my understanding as well. Initiations that take place with us all, have to do with how we have become more of our true selves." says Megan-spirit bear.

Dollygal belly begins to tremble and shake. Then suddenly a stomach full of laughter burst out of her mouth.

Megan-spirit bear and Morgan-truth bear suddenly begin to laugh uncontrollably, and then Professor Boo and Mr. Protégé.

Then Peacock and Serpent began to fall under the spell of this magical laughter, that traveled as the breath of air through "The Great Garden".

Then some tree people arrived from the village, excited to bring forth a new story about the laughter that guided them—

"We were embraced by this laughter on our travels from the village. We set out to follow your steps, but everything seemed different. The laughter came upon us all, and we followed the laughter here." says the joyful tree villagers.

Still full of laughter, Megan-spirit bear and Morgan-truth bear embrace their people with hugs—

"I think it's time we travel back to the village. We have a lot of work to do with the new understanding of our ancestors and our Queen – Dollygal." says Morgan-truth bear as he kisses her hand.

Dollygal giggles—

"I will use my new wings to fly above and lead the way." Megan-spirit bear cheerfully speaks.

"I think we should do the same Mr. Protege. It's time we travel back into town and start preparing for the school classes and so forth.

I'm sure you both would agree with me on this Mr. Peacock and Mr. Serpent?" says Professor Boo.

"Most definitely Professor Boo. Thank you so much for all that you do, and you too Mr. Protégé." says Peacock.

"Indeed Sir, my brother and I don't know what we would do without your help. I truly mean that." says Serpent as he extends his hand out to Professor Boo.

Mr. Protege cheerfully turns his attention to Dollygal and says—

"Dollygal, I just want to say that I am not confused or upset (like your brother Serpent), by you not wanting to speak about your experience. So, I am not going to ask you that ever again." says Mr. Protege.

"Thanks, Mr. Protege, I would rather help all of you experience what I did. Maybe we can all work on that together." says Dollygal.

OOOHHHH!!!... I didn't think of that. That would be fantastic Dollygal!" Mr. Protégé's ears flopped up and down as he jumps around with excitement.

"That would definitely be a class worthwhile in the "School of Intention". I'll get to work on the next curriculum right away.

We will leave you three now and travel back to town. I am very sure that there is some unfinished business to be discussed between you all.

We will surely miss our lovely old friend and teacher; Mrs. Engirdle. She has left us with many wonderful teachings from the "School of Intention". says Professor Boo.

Peacock sits on a big rock and sits Dollygal on his lap. While Serpent sits on a rock next to them. He glares at Dollygal with his left eyebrow higher than the other.

"We are waiting to be told something extremely profound. Go ahead little sister, spit it out." says Serpent.

"I'm going to agree with Serpent on this one Dollygal. It's like I can fill it inside me." says Peacock.

"Wait... before we get into something very deep... I would just like to say that I was not confused nor was I upset about you not speaking about your personal experience, as Mr. Protege so rudely pointed out." says Serpent.

"Ha... Ha... Ha... Serpent, I was there, and you were very annoyed. Ha... Ha... Ha..."

"As I recall, brother of mine, it didn't sit too well with you either, Ha... Ha... Ha..."

"Hey, I understand completely why you would be anxious to know. Your little sister disappears into a mountain, then only to return later. Of course, everyone would want to know what happened!" says Dollygal, as she motions her arms around.

"Yes, Yes... so tell us what happened little sister." Peacock and Serpent replied simultaneously.

"Please don't ask me that, but I will help you have your own experience." says Dollygal.

Serpent covers his face trying not to be annoyed.

Dollygal giggles while covering her mouth with her hand.

"OK, let's continue this profound conversation Dollygal.

What's happening now?" says Peacock.

"You and brother Serpent have assignments to do. You are to build a Rainbow Bridge for me. I can show you where to build it.

It is already here, but you cannot see it yet. It is the bridge that brought me back here.

Once you start to build, you will see for yourselves." says Dollygal.

"You can see it now? What does it look like?" says Serpent.

Dollygal oval shaped eyes widen as she speaks—

"Well, it is a very old brown bridge coming out of the ever-flowing waterfalls. It's been unseen here for a very long time – until now.

All colors of the rainbow created this bridge, which would eventually be used to unify and bring together—the physical world and celestial worlds.

Peacock and Serpent look at one another with confusion—

"We have been trusted to bring forth such a task as this?!"says Peacock.

"Yes, both of you have been chosen to complete the Rainbow Bridge for all to see." Dollygal smiles.

"But we cannot see the bridge as you do little sister! What will we use for lumber?

How big is this bridge?

There's a lot of planning and preparation involved in order to complete such a task as this one." says Serpent.

"Once you start to build, then you will see it yourself. Please brother Peacock and brother Serpent, sit and let me tell a story to you both." Dollygal takes her brothers by the hands and sits cross-legged as her brother sits on big rocks.

"When I was a little girl,

Serpent interrupts—

"You still are a little girl, sort of anyway!"

"Please continue Dollygal." says Peacock as he glares at Serpent.

"When I was a little girl, I had a dream about Father. He said to me,

"Dollygal, when the time is right, I want you to uncover and bring forth something very special I have hidden behind my office."

"What office did he have brother Peacock, brother Serpent?"

"The small carriage house was his office." says Peacock.

"Huh... you mean his home away from home. He spent all his time experimenting with everything." says Serpent.

"We boarded that place up a long time ago. I have not been in it since then." says Peacock.

"Our father was a self-proclaimed time traveler, and he was a great storyteller, Dollygal." says Peacock.

"Indeed, he was a storyteller... Ha... Ha... Ha... Remember that story he told us as children, so we would stay out of his office?" Serpent laughs loudly.

"What was the story about, brother Serpent.' says Dollygal.

"He said, he had time-traveled to a special place and brought back something very rare. He forbade us from ever playing inside or around the carriage house which he used as his office. That is where he spent most of his time - day and night." says Serpent as he suddenly pauses.

"He said we would find it very useful one day. But only at the perfect time." says Peacock.

Peacock and Serpent eyes quickly look at one another in amazement.

Simultaneously, they speak the same words as unified in one mind.

Stuff for the bridge is behind the carriage house. It's been here this whole time!!!

"I'm feeling we are having yet another quite profound and extraordinary moment here Serpent. I have no words to say, but the beauty that I feel inside is about to overcome me. I'll need your help to get me through it" says Peacock as he covers his face with his hands.

"I understand dear brother, and I feel the same. I feel such an abundance of beauty and gratitude as if it's inside my body, and it's very overwhelming. But I wouldn't change a thing about how I'm feeling. Does this even make any sense to you at all?!" Serpent says as he laughs out loud.

"Yeah, it does, I feel the same. I would not change a moment of where we came from, and what we have gone through because it brought us to this amazing moment right now, brother of mine." says Peacock.

Dollygal stands up in front of her brothers—

"Now you know how I feel. You both experienced awesome beauty in a new way, and that is the initiation you have both earned." says Dollygal.

"You know Dollygal, we are your brothers here to help and protect you. But I think it's time Serpent and I acknowledge that we need our little sister's help and guidance, because she is the one with the "Gift" that can help us develop our gifts." says Peacock.

"I think we can all use a group hug at this moment." says Serpent

Dollygal, Peacock, and the Serpent hug was a very strong hug. It's so strong that Dollygal began to shake and tremble. Then her belly released big joyful laughter springing forth out of her mouth and into the air.

The laughter softly tiptoed across the lake, tickling the trees along the way. Then intertwined within the waterfalls, thrust itself upon the mountain, ultimately springing forth from the top, then rapidly immersing itself throughout the entire "Great Garden".

"Whoa, are you OK brother Peacock, brother Serpent?"

"Yes, we are just fine, right Serpent?" says Peacock.

"OOOhhh!!! Indeed we are all okay." says Serpent.

They excitedly look at one another and speak simultaneously—

'Did we see all of that my brother?" "Yes, we did... yes, we did...!!!"

"Dollygal, we got a glimpse into the journey you took. Our connection with you is stronger now." says Peacock.

"I am astounded once again, my little sister. But now we have work to do, brother of mine." says Peacock.

I am ready." says Serpent.

"We will allow ourselves to be guided by a great power in the "Great Garden", to build the sacred bridge." says Peacock.

Then two white glowing balls of light appear before Peacock and Serpent.

"Whoa!!! What are these balls of light, Dollygal?" says Peacock.

"I've never seen these within the Garden before." says Serpent.

"They have always been here, now they will help you both build the bridge. Consider them your new friends." says Dollygal, with a big smile and a wink of an eye.

"Let's go home. You need rest little sister. You have a big job to do for everyone."

"Shall we take the scenic long route or shortcut to the castle?" says Serpent as he chuckles with laughter.

"Let's take the long route, then you guys can tell me what you saw from the experience." Dollygal gleefully speaks with a big smile and wide eyes.

The brothers looks at one another, then at the Dollygal, and answers simultaneously—

"Dollygal, please don't ask us that..."

Dollygal's giggles, busted into a loud and joyous, belly-holding laughter. It was heard all throughout "The Great Garden" and Lovelyville...

The End...

and a New Beginning...

EPILOGUE

"The Great Garden" and "The rainbow bridge"

Lovelyville people are now Allowing themselves to experience the joyful and insightful connection to the voice of "The Great Garden and the new manifestation of "The rainbow bridge." They have much work to do in order to believe what they are now experiencing... IS TRUE...IS REAL....

So, the journey of the mind continues to elevate them to new thoughts...

Unity and order are now leading them in the way to the most magnificent journey of their lives...

Be the peace... Be the love... Bepeacelove!

ABOUT THE AUTHOR

My name is Darlene Cannon.

I am a new writer on the scene and I believe that anything is possible and nothing is impossible...

I am a deep believer in the power of Love.

I am a true fan of a lot of great writers, story tellers that bring forth movies and books that challenge the mundane world view.

Be peace love...

Contact information:

Emails: Darlene@bepeacelove.com

Darlene@dollygalpeacockandtheserpent.com

Website: Bepeacelove.com